"Perhaps the most distinctive stories in Alexandra Kleeman's *Intimations* are the brilliantly crafted nightmares about the dissolving of reality, but there is also everything here from an elegant Victorian tale of a feral child to a witty disquisition on the mouths of angels. A memory of childhood with an invented sister is told by way of a 'brief history of weather,' a romantic breakup by way of apocalyptic metaphors. This is ambitious, imaginative writing of the highest quality."

—Robert Coover, author of *The Public Burning*

Intimations

ALSO BY ALEXANDRA KLEEMAN

You Too Can Have a Body Like Mine

INTIMATIONS

Stories

ALEXANDRA

KLEEMAN

HARPER

An Imprint of HarperCollins*Publishers*

HarperCollins books may be purchased for educational, business, or sales promotional use. For information, please email the Special Markets Department at SPsales@ harpercollins.com.

Versions of the following stories have been previously published: "Fairy Tale" in *The Paris Review*; "Lobster Dinner" in *Gulf Coast*; "A Brief History of Weather" in *Conjunctions*; "Choking Victim" in *The New Yorker*; "Intimation" in *The Last Magazine*; "Fake Blood" in *Zoetrope: All-Story*; "Hylomorphosis" in *Conjunctions*; "Rabbit Starvation" in *BOMB*; "You, Disappearing" in *Guernica*.

FIRST EDITION

Designed by Fritz Metsch

Library of Congress Cataloging-in-Publication Data has been applied for.

ISBN 978-0-06238870-4

16 17 18 19 20   RRD   10 9 8 7 6 5 4 3 2 1

To Alex Gilvarry

Contents

I.

II.

III.

I.

Fairy Tale

I was sitting at a long table with a lot of nice things on it. There was a large pitcher of water with an ornate handle that looked like it was made of real silver, and there were forks and spoons. There were apples and small, round appetizers, and a big dead cooked goose. There were so many things that the table underneath was eclipsed entirely; the visible objects obscured even more food, more tableware beneath.

My mother and father were sitting next to each other on the long side of the table, and a man I didn't recognize at all was sitting next to them. I sat across on the other end, alone.

I was looking at all of the things and trying to notice connections between them. Why this table, why now? Why these things and not others? Many of the things were round. Except the goose. I tried looking from object to object: fork, butter, spinach, hand, napkin, apple, cup.

It was then that I noticed that none of the others seated at the table were looking at the table or its contents. They were all looking at me. They were looking continuously, there was no sense that they would soon be looking away. They had these looks on their faces. Especially the man. He had a look like he just would never ever get enough of looking. His eyes were like two little identical stones, the bare minimum of a face, just enough to make you look twice to check if you were looking at a person. You were announcing your engagement, said my father helpfully.

To who? I asked.

I felt a strange sense of ownership for all the objects on the table, yet I did not want to claim them.

To us, they said. All of you? I said.

No, only me, said the man in the button-up shirt, who I did not recognize.

I find it increasingly difficult to speak of my feelings at will.

I am announcing my engagement to you? I asked, gesturing at him. Yes, exactly, he said, looking satisfied. It seemed impossible to phrase the question in a way that would yield a perfectly unambiguous answer.

Who am I engaged to? I asked.

To me, he said, no longer looking satisfied.

The whole situation felt as unreal as something could while also feeling sorely, mortally dangerous. It seemed to draw strength from my speech, as in: the more I spoke within it, accepting its premises, the more I spoke into it without screaming at it, the more it made me whoever this position demanded.

Has anyone carved the goose? I asked. We'd better carve it before it gets cold, or hard. Before it reverses. We'd better do something before it changes.

Stay on topic, darling, and try to be polite, my mother replied. We were having a discussion, and it's only a family discussion if you participate.

There was no way out. All the doors were far away and in the line of sight. I don't think it's unrelated, I said, or I don't think it's impolite. I am going to make one or both of those arguments, I said.

My suitor looked at his watch.

I think you're being difficult, my mother replied. I think you should sit down and finish the announcement you started. There's ice cream for after the announcement, and it's already in the dishes melting.

The doorbell rang and I went to the door.

Standing outside was a man who looked almost entirely unfamiliar, like someone I had met maybe once through an acquaintance or circumstantial friend. Hi, he said. Oh hi, I replied. Who are you? I wanted to say. But instead I just looked at him, at his medium-size mouth, his large-size nose, his normal-size face.

I'm your boyfriend? he said helpfully, holding up a fistful of flowers.

I would have asked a follow-up question but instead I felt myself begin to slow down as if I had been filled up with damp sand. I thought about the person in the other room who said he was my fiancé, and I wondered if I had been designed to function within this situation or, instead, to somehow undo it.

I remember a proverb that I once found carved into the body of an old tree: whether the knife falls on the melon or the melon on the knife, the melon suffers.

Oh, hi, I said. Sweetheart?

I guided him into the kitchen and pointed him to the table. Mother, father, fiancé, I said, this is my boyfriend. My fiancé immediately began to look uncomfortable, but did not voice this discomfort except by a soft gurgling sound in the throat. I seated the boyfriend across from the fiancé and watched. Perhaps they would cancel each other out. How do you do, said the boyfriend to each member of the table in turn. He shook my father's hand, kissed my mother's, and nodded sharply at my fiancé. The gurgling escalated, but my mother politely switched on the dishwasher, and soon we heard mostly the sound of machinery rather than that of a person's feelings surfacing.

He has some manners, said my father to no one in particular.

Perhaps we should carve the goose? said my boyfriend, rifling through the pile of silverware on the table. Where's the knife? he asked. I remember an infomercial for a set of knives, their blades fortified with diamond powder. They were advertised as *the only knives you'll love to need, need to love, need to need, etc.!* In the advertisement, anonymous hands wielded shiny shiny blades that chopped through butter and animal bone as if they were the same thing, through ice and tendon and untreated wood as if there was no difference between anything in the world—only a slight variation in grain, visible once something has been split in half.

All eyes turned toward me, and it was at this moment that I realized I was in my own house, and these things were my things.

I just don't know, I said to everything.

At that moment, men were beginning to file into the room from somewhere else; they took positions in the corners of the room or in strategic corridors. Strange furnishings, they filled the space without filling the silence. They shuffled and stared, their silence had an eagerness.

. . .

Won't you introduce us? they said.

I began to form a sentence beginning These are, but I lacked the words to complete it.

Who are you? I asked.

We're your boyfriends, partners, paramours, they responded in a broken chorus.

I thought I would go first to check on the door, I must have forgotten to shut it. More might come if I didn't close it quickly. There was a tension between the demands of the suitors and the capacities of the home, the structure of furnishings, plates, food that I had woken into. At the same time, there was a strange reciprocity between them, as the presence of a suitor seemed to demand the performance of hospitality, even as the presence of surplus plates, chairs, napkins, seemed to draw more strangers into the house.

I arrived to find the entryway empty, save for a man in what appeared to be a uniform stepping across the threshold.

I'm just the postman, he said. Oh, I said, please come in.

. . . Since you broke up with me, he finished.

. . .

Oh, I said. There was a stiff feeling in the air. If only I could remember one thing about him, I could say it out loud. Nice shirt, I said.

Yes—since you broke up with me, he said, as if I'd know what he meant.

There was a hazy damp film in his eyes that I recognized from emotions in old movies, projected large on darkened screens.

But, then, you'd hardly remember, would you? he said bitterly.

What sort of person was I? I had a rich store of memories, recent ones and much older ones, their edges rubbed smooth over time. I could remember that I was certified to perform CPR and that I spent summer afternoons in third grade swimming at the quarry, where they sold ice cream bars shaped like the heads of cartoon animals. But I had no idea who this person might be, or who any of the people might be who sat at that table and watched me at the door and claimed to have feelings not exactly for me, but at me. When they smiled, the skin around their eyes and mouths bunched up. I had the distinct sense they were all made of the same material, by someone who owned a big bolt of fleshy cloth. At some point I must have met them, loved them, had fine times. But now all they evoked was a sense of responsibility, a vague and resentful crust.

When I led this new man back to the table, the suitors had already begun to compete in earnest.

I'm her fiancé, one said. I'm her boyfriend, said another. Me too, said the third. They glared at each other across the table, and one took a roll from another's plate and ate it with anger. There doesn't have to be a conflict between those things, I said hopefully. They glared at me. Was I going to have to choose? Here, now, in front of all these people, in an exposed and public scene? And if they made me choose, how could I? I didn't know anything about any of them, in fact I could barely tell them apart. When I looked at them I struggled to note subtle differences in hairstyle, which I cross-referenced to well-known television actors with distinct names that I applied mentally to each suitor for sorting purposes, though I kept these names within quotation marks to remind myself that they were only temporary. "Patrick" "David" "Jason" "Rob."

"Michael" "Marco" "Carl" "Jack." Most of the time when I looked at them I couldn't even see their faces or if they had faces: Was this Love?

I turned to my mother. I wanted to ask: Couldn't I just choose none of them? Swiveling her head sharply, she gave me a look with her lips tightened. She breathed quickly in and out, nostrils flared. I knew the answer would be no.

. . .

The structural similarity of men, and their ability to be represented both as ideal, like Leonardo's Vitruvian Man, and as average. Man being the measure of all things, and therefore a sort of standard and interchangeable unit of length, breadth, intelligence, emotion. We could lay them end to end to measure the distance between the continents, the distance to the moon. We could use them to calculate the weight of the weather, or to buy things at the grocery store. With such an abundance of men, we could gauge anything we chose.

I knew I was behaving badly. I could barely attend to the words on a sonic level. The suitor on the left who kept trying to hold my hand, I had offended by replacing my hand in his with a dinner roll. As they went around the table listing nouns and adjectives that corresponded, somehow, to whole persons, I tried to focus my thinking not on the world of men, the superfluity of men, the community of men, or their etiquette and social contracts, but on men in the particular. Men replete with difference.

All right, said my mother. Who will you be choosing?

Well, he brought flowers, I said, pointing at the one who had brought flowers.

The flowers in their wrapping gave off a trapped and fragrant odor.

. . .

It's true, he said, standing up. And I have to confess, I love you very much. I think you're perfect for me. But I will tell you something soon that will make you wish you could change your mind.

Why don't you step into the kitchen to talk this through? my father suggested. It sounds personal.

Okay, I said.

He took me by the elbow and directed me out of the room, turning back briefly to wink roguishly at the table of parents and men that watched us still. I tried to wave or gesture apologetically, as an apology for my own lapse of manners, but with his thumb on the inner joint and his palm wrapped firmly around the back, I found I could do little more than wriggle the limb.

In the kitchen he turned to me and held me close. He brushed a strand of hair from my face and traced the jawline with two long fingers. And you? he asked, smiling softly. How are you feeling, my darling?

I'm confused, I answered.

Yes, yes, he said thoughtfully. You want to know my feelings, my constitution. You want to know that I care about you, you want assurances that I love you, that I think of you deeply, he said.

. . .

I thought about this, which seemed less than I actually wanted to know, but also a step toward knowing anything at all. That sounds good, I said.

Well, yes, it sounds good, he replied, chuckling, and it is most certainly true, but it should also be known to you, as it is known to myself, that I came here with the intent to kill you.

What? I asked.

Also, I came here to kill you, he clarified.

He was already rooting around in the kitchen drawers, looking for a knife to push through my chest. It wasn't the right time to bring this up. Maybe there would be a right time later.

Are you really the only person who doesn't have a knife, any knife of any sort, in their kitchen? he asked with a note of irritation in his voice.

That's what it looks like, I said. I meant this in an earnest way, free of sarcasm, but I could tell I was sounding like a bitch.

Listen to you two, you sound like an old married couple, said a suitor who had wandered into the kitchen by accident. He chuckled to himself.

. . .

Help me, I said to him.

Help you what? he answered.

Escape from this guy, I said, who is trying to kill me.

Help you, *please*, is what I was waiting to hear, said the suitor wryly.

A few feet away, my killer looked at his watch.

The man I had chosen was going to find something sharp and come after me and stab me with it. He would not tell me his reasons and in the meantime I would have to tell him mine, my reasons for not wanting to be stabbed. Being stabbed would interfere with the general harmony of my body, with its function, with its status as self-containing vessel, whole and protective. It would interfere with my nervous system and my circulatory system, with my respiratory system and, to a lesser extent, my immune system. It would spring a leak in me. It would leave me open to the world.

The helpful suitor, in the meantime, had located a door to another room.

In here, he said.

. . .

Now we were in here. In here was my bedroom, still dec-
orated with the poster of Minnie Mouse that I had owned
since middle school. Didn't I ever get rid of anything?

Lock the door, I said. Like this? he said, wiggling the knob.
No, lock it, I said. Lock it so it can't be opened, I explained
further.

He looked distracted. Use the lock, I said, more sharply and
loudly.

You don't have to snap at me, he said. I went to the lock and
turned it, but it went around and around. He had found the
only room in the house with a nonfunctional lock. I heard
footsteps slowly coming up the stairs. They stopped in front
of the other bedroom and then the bathroom. Then they
stopped in front of my door.

You'd better let me in, he said.

The door's locked, I said. You'd never get through. I was
bluffing. I needed more details to make the lie convincing,
but I was all out of words. There was a long silence and I
hoped that he would not try the knob.

Well, it doesn't matter, he said thoughtfully. Because I found
a knife, a really sharp one. And it can reach you through

the door even if it's locked. As long as you're standing here talking to me.

I hesitated. Was he bluffing?

Is it a long knife? I asked through the door.

Yes, he said.

I don't believe you, I said through the door.

Why's that? he said.

I thought hard. Because I would have heard it when you came up the stairs, I said, hoping that he would let it go. I don't think that's true, he said.

Fine, then tap it against the doorknob, I said. Let me hear it.

Clink, clink, he said.

No, I said, I'm not buying it. Okay, he said, but I'm not going to believe that your door is locked either. If it were locked, you wouldn't be talking to me here. You'd be over at the window behind you, trying to find a way out. I felt a pit in my chest. He was right. I should have been there trying to get out. Instead I had wasted that time trying to talk about the situation. I looked behind me. The man with the short hair was sitting on my bed, reading one of my books.

. . .

Then the one I had chosen burst into the room. He was holding an armful of things he had found in the linen closet, which, I assumed, he was planning on using as weapons. First he took an armful of mixed towels and washcloths and attempted to drive them into my back. Then he grabbed a collapsible laundry hamper and threw it in the direction of my head. He picked up some containers of fabric softener and lobbed them at me, and then tried repeatedly to jam a feather duster through my chest. He picked up a long cushion that had come from the couch.

At this rate it would take forever.

He paused, breathing heavily. Okay, look, he said. I give up. I love you and I don't remember why I'm trying to kill you. Can we just start over? I thought about it. What would we do? I asked. We could watch a movie, he suggested.

I didn't know what to say. I knew I had a big choice to make. I could let it all go and try to love him, try to trust him, try to make something lasting and good. He obviously had strong feelings for me or about me. And he wasn't being so bad right now. We could build something sturdy, beautiful. Or I could try to make a dash for the door by crawling under the dining room table.

There was a good chance that he would kill me later, either way.

. . .

I dove under the table and scrambled toward the door.

He was still behind me, cursing over. the fallen chairs
that lay before him and the ten-foot lead I had. But when
I reached for the knob, it wouldn't turn. The lock was on
the outside. Who ever heard of the lock for a door being on
the outside? It would be up to another, possibly a total and
complete stranger, to decide whether you'd ever be allowed
to leave.

I knew it was time to run again. He was looking around the
room for a better weapon, and he would probably find it. I
was so tired. I just wanted to curl up with someone, anyone,
even him, and sleep until work on Monday. I wanted to feel
someone's, anyone's, hands on me, even if it was in that way
I hate, the fingers all over my face and jaw.

Lobster Dinner

1

The lobsters were dead in a pile and no longer a danger to us. They were dead in a pile and their shells were not brown not red not blue, but the color of eyes, both yours and mine. We ate them to destroy them but a murmuring came, nevertheless, from their empty carapaces, uncracked. The lobsters with their soft, hissing voices and their words like air escaping a punctured tire. We ate them to destroy them all but suddenly we felt sad and empty and overly full. I turned to you and for the first time told you I was in love. The lobsters were dead in a pile and with a froth on their shells they waited and watched us undress each other. They no longer made the hostile lobster sounds, they no longer threatened us in tiny words with the destruction of our species but waited there dead with eyes that looked little different from the eyes of the living. There on the shore the sun glowed and our love was indestructible, though the sea washed up a strange red froth. The lobsters were in piles and they no longer moved, but some of them did and were alive still and in their movements within the pile they made the heap writhe like water boiling in a pot. We had eaten the lobsters to forestall our own destruction, but it became clear that nothing would. I resettled myself on the sand and leaned back against you, and I closed my eyes, stroking your leg and your large right claw, and I was at rest at last.

2

Holiday in Cape Cod. Lucy spreads the beach blanket on the hot sand, and I jump on to avoid burning the soles of my feet. Susan is slathering sunscreen on the exposed segments of her body, as the gulls circle over us all. We play paddle-ball and catch and the little red rubber sphere traces out a path among us three. I walk down to the seam of shore and sea and practice digging small holes with my feet, holes that fill immediately with water. Does water lurk everywhere, just below the surface, or only here?

I see you farther upshore, fully clothed, watching me carve hopeless marks in the sand. I see a giant lobster, the size of a beach blanket, stranded at the shoreline. It looks a tender pink. You see me seeing the lobster, but you do nothing. The lobster strokes desperately but it only digs itself farther in, its legs slap at the wet dark sand. A common misconception is that a lobster screams when boiled; actually the whistling sound is steam escaping the shell. I go over to the giant lobster, not wishing to touch it. But I take up a stick of drift-wood and I will wedge it from the sand, roll it toward the water.

I go over and briefly it stops struggling and in this still moment I think it may be grateful, waiting to be helped. I am nudging the shard under and under its belly to lift and overhead the gulls go wild. Now the blood is gushing, blue blood, frothing all over the gulls that swoop in to eat from its belly, eat of its belly, it was too tender to move and it is emptying quick. My stick still sticks in it, the stick now blue the gulls blue my hands are blue, blue is everywhere I look except you. You are pale and clean, watching me from afar. You look queasy.

That sound: was it a whistle, a hiss, or a scream? From the ocean come thousands upon thousands of lobsters and they are not whistling or hissing or screaming but are whispering one word over and over again, over and over and over.

3

"I'll have the Lobster in Cream Sauce," Susan says, tilting her head this way and that at the menu. "But please make certain the seafood is of local origin: we have all traveled too far to dine on imported creatures."

Plunge two lobsters each weighing two pounds into the boiling water, quickly so they die at once; break off the large claws and set them in the center of a saucepan. Douse in white wine and water, add bay leaves, parsley, and onion and boil for twenty minutes, then pull apart the tails, strain the creamy innards, and fry the remainder in butter. Moisten with lobster stock and add shallots, cream, and brandy. Cut the bodies in slices and lay the shells at the sides, the heads facing up toward you, directly toward you, and pointed away from the sea.

. . .

Lucy licks her lips, studies the menu. "I'd like the Lobster *à la Bordelaise*. With extra wedges of lemon and some Tabasco, please."

In white wine, with a broth based on lobster flesh, simmered with diced carrots, onions, and potatoes. The lobster must be fresh, unfrozen, caught from cold water that hardens the shell. A lobster is sweetest and full of the richest flesh right before a molt, when the shell is at its most protective. Before it has shed its sense of safety.

And for me? A cup of the corn chowder, with a small salad. Dressing on the side.

Susan looks at me with a combination of amusement and scorn. "Oh, Anne-Marie. Only you would attempt vegetarianism on the Cape, in the summer. Why not live a little, eat the best? After all, you are what you eat."

But I am not.

4

What a beautiful day as thousands and thousands of lobsters skitter up from the water, whispering their single word over and over again as the sky blues brightly overhead. What a beautiful color staining the swollen breasts of the gulls as they argue over the last contents of the great lobster, nearly fainting from their own fullness. Susan and Lucy look over at me from a distance and they put down their red rubber ball, uncertain. We were to take a sunset stroll to the leeward side of the cove, hand in hand, as when we were children, but now a sound comes from the sea and I sense our plans must be reconsidered.

The sound rises like the whistling of a teakettle but breaks into a shriek, a single beautiful tone that pierces the sea breeze like a knife, cracks it like a mallet, and when it has gone on long enough I can begin to hear the word whispered beneath. By the time the lobsters have begun to kill us, I recognize it distinctly.

The lobsters take down a healthy athletic type, they take him behind the knees and he crumples like a doll. The lobsters with their clumsy claws are terrible in droves, the sun glistens off their backs and they are a wave, a tide, a drowning of speckled brown and red crawling over the faces of people. I look down at my hands covered in blue and tell myself this is not happening, but of course it is. They fight their way into the mouths and down the airways of vacationers of all ages, indiscriminate.

And you are running toward me while the lobsters are killing us all, your hair ruffled in the breeze and the sun glistening off your smooth shoulders, and you are mouthing something, shouting it, something I cannot hear over the screams of lobsters and of people. You reach me and then you whisper in my ear that we must kill them all. I nod slowly as you grab one of the largest in your hands and tear it in half. You hold one of the halves out to me, it drips blue on the warm, soft sand. I take it in my hands tentatively, like it could hurt me, and I bite down.

5

So full. Full of lobster meat and the sadness of the lobster meat. Full of the feeling of having cracked hundreds upon hundreds of precious shells. Full of the sound and the sight of destruction, the lobsters dead in a pile, some of them with lipstick marks on their empty husks. Their voices piled up on one another. I felt a whispering coming from deep within my belly, the voices not yet at rest, and they said in a tone sympathetic and unsympathetic at the same time, Next Next Next. "Well," I said, "what do we do next?" "Lobster dinner?" he asked, chuckling a little as if I ought to be chuckling with him as well. And as he leaned in to kiss me, my eye saw his open mouth grow larger and larger until it seemed it could swallow me whole.

The Dancing-Master

1

The body of Victor Tallon bends both of its knees on the downbeat, sinking and suddenly halting, like a toy abandoned by a child. Legs crooked, he remains there too long, squatting shallowly in the midst of what had once been a passable plié. The stiff arms hold their shape, suspended as if from threads extending invisibly into the heavens. After several seconds, the finely positioned arms begin to quiver.

From where I stand, I watch this tremor grow bolder, as I watch also the eyes beginning to brim with a considerable quantity of tears. He moistens rapidly. His emptied mouth gapes toward the audience like a dark hole deep, deep in the woods. Meanwhile, the music has already moved on, marching toward the fourth bar, though a strain of hesitancy creeps into the notes as it occurs to each of the players that they might soon be ordered to slow down, or to cease entirely.

I give him a stern appraisal, from the slack mouth to the slackening hips. He should now be executing the *élevé*, but it is all terribly wrong. He tilts left somewhat and looks as though he might topple. Though he has been perfectly still for the last few minutes, poised mid-sequence for fear of making an error, now his legs begin to wriggle in place. It occurs to me that he might fall upon all fours and make a dash for the palace doors, straight for the elegant foyer and its elegant escape, fleeing like a dog from a promise of certain punishment. Such a turn would not take me by surprise: Victor Tallon is a savage, and holds a coward's attitude toward the art of dance. But when I lower my hand gently to the rod at my hip, he pitches forward and releases a gasp, a spasm of fearful sound. The neck protruding from his collar and coat is pink with fear, twisted round like a wrung goose. Then he resumes his choreography, proceeding as instructed through the rise, the jeté, another plié, another *élevé*, another light and airy kick. For one such as he, accustomed to the harsh admonitions of the wilderness, only a similar harshness will stir him to civilized action.

I look to the braggart philosopher Portesquieu to measure his response, but he does not meet my eye. Victor continues to sway a bit too much for my liking, giving the elegant *chacotte* an unseemly teetering quality. However, it must be said that his posture is impeccable.

2

Young Victor Tallon wandered into our village three years and thirty-seven days ago, wearing upon his head a flap of filthy linen made more vile by the matted teats of hair hung beneath it. The physician who examined him estimated his age at sixteen years, though with his stunted height and well-developed teeth he could have been a man closer to my own. When we realized that he was more than a beggar— far more, by way of being far less—we descended upon him

as children upon a sack of sweets. Not only was he unable
to give us an account of himself, his name, origin, occupation, the name of his father, the occupation of his father,
the whereabouts of his mother, etcetera, he was unable to
account for anything at all. To our questions and threats, he
made a soft chuffing sound, followed by a sort of attempt to
bite the air, snapping at it and gnashing his teeth as though
he had seized upon some delicacy. Men and women of all
ages and ranks, we convened upon the town square to see
this empty vessel, to gather around him, to lift up his lips
to examine his gums, to explore his sensitivity to prodding
and loud sounds.

That night in the tavern, the philosopher Portesquieu ad-
dressed me before all present. Dancing-master, he said from
a mouth stained with meat, why do you not try your hand
at reforming the wild young man? You claim that you are
a favorite of the court, surely some official would commend
him to your custody, to teach him the essentials of modern
thought and comportment. Perhaps knowing the proper ex-
ecution of the gavotte would help the boy make sense of the
world.

Amid his laughter, I reflected upon the many spiritual
benefits that a mastery of the dance could offer. A firm
knowledge of the social dances—invented for pleasure yet
placed in the service of the public good—could benefit the
poor savage in both mind and body. For if the elegant gestures of the dance spring from a deeply cultivated sense
of intelligence and propriety, it is clear that knowledge of
these gestures would cultivate the appropriate intelligence
in its practitioner.

It is to this end that I took young Victor on as my own student, and to this end that he performs the steps as I have taught him, in the order I have taught him, before this audience: the audience that will affirm his civilization. It is for this reason that he rotates with his left arm extended and his right gently curved—performing the court dances like a gracious and sensible man. Although he does not yet understand what any of those words mean.

3

Victor executes a magnificent bow in the center of the hall. He bends before a bramble of eyes, convened to witness the degree to which bodily form may supplant a long history of mental formlessness. He is a portrait of health and good grooming: his eyes and gums no longer ooze. Atop his head, he wears a wig of coppery curls that suits him as though it were his own from birth, and upon which the sides have been pinned back in the style of the moment, and to prevent him from chewing at it. The fitted coat and collar make the most of his shape, so much so that the least choosy of the court ladies titter to each other as he passes by. As he takes his first step into the second prepared dance, a minuet choreographed to the playing of flute, tambourine, and harpsichord, I am pleased to note that every possible sign of good breeding has been stamped onto his surface, wrought in his flesh. Not a thing is out of place as he glides forward into the first movement, but for the composition of the face.

Set back within a recess of the coppery wig, two eyes twitch back and forth rapidly, like finches traversing a small cage. They give the appearance of little creatures trying to see past the glorious billows of auburn waves, to see a way out. Below, Victor's small red mouth pops open and closed, open and closed, a vestige of his former penchant for gnawing at the air. Beyond the red rims, teeth that are blinding white: purer, whiter than any I have seen in the mouths of those raised on more cultivated foods.

I frown to myself. In his treatise on the history of dance, Cahusec writes: "The different affections of the soul are the origin of gestures, and the dance, which is made up of them, is consequently the art of executing them with grace and proportion relative to the affections they express." Yet I know that this particular gesture originates in young Victor Tallon's desire to have his chewing-toy returned to him, a base desire reflective of his regression toward savagery. Earlier that day he slyly tried to hand over a piece of chipped wood when I came to recoup it from him before the performance. When I persisted, he made attempts to demonstrate his affection for the toy, miming his pleasure at gnawing upon it, showing that it could be concealed completely within his mouth.

Rooting around among the feverish little points, the wet and roiling tongue, I explained to him that, invisible though it might be, the simple knowledge of its presence would rot the occasion from within, destroying my satisfaction entirely.

4

Young Victor arrived at my door a dwarfish creature, freshly shorn and clothed in a length of linen. He resembled a boy, but only in shape. He lacked a boy's liveliness and capacity for joy, he would not be enticed by bright scraps of cloth or the antics of dogs at play. To most of the world he was calloused: he did not turn toward the sound of a human voice, nor did he seem to note particularly the difference between a well-enunciated sentence and a hacking cough. He loved to eat and to lie about unbothered and to gnaw upon the objects whose names and functions I attempted over and over to teach him. To all else he was indifferent. I placed his head and hands in the proper position for attending to my instruction, only to look back and find them slumping back into his customary untidy heap. There were times when I watched him rolling around belly-up in the pastures, chewing upon a convenient branch, and despaired that I would ever teach him even the meanest of jigs.

While with most beginning students I would first impart an understanding of the names and qualities of the most common courtly dances, young Victor required a most intricate and time-consuming education. I was faced with the problem of persuading him to pay any notice at all to higher forms of activity, for he was inclined to an eventless life spent supine in various corners of his chamber. Once, I performed an exquisite series of *balancés* for his benefit, to which he responded by gnawing on my headpiece while I was occupied. In rejoinder, I removed from his daily routine those few things that he favored—food, flowers, and chewable items. I set in their place a system of tutorials directed toward teaching him the most elevated of concepts and behaviors, which I believed he would interest himself in were he not continually able to please himself by putting objects into his mouth. It is in this manner that societies have caused their own advancement: by starving themselves of ready satisfactions, they stir their appetite for finer sustenance.

Unfortunately, my benevolent deprivations created in Victor only the most rudimentary physical effects. With movements and sounds, he complained of his hunger and boredom, of the disuse of his mouth, while I lectured on, discoursing on the subjects of agriculture, ancestry, the difference between present-day architectural ratios and those employed by the ancients. The only tutorial that attracted his attention was my explanation of crying, a sort of footnote to a more extensive lecture on the relationship of emotions to gesture. Victor watched with open mouth as I mimed sadness, even greater sadness, and then indicated with my fingers the streaming of tears down my face. When I made the noise itself, the gutted syllables of a man weeping, he leapt up, clapping with his hands and chuffing madly. As I tried to calm him, he roved about the property uttering sobs and palpating his eyes that they might tear more readily. I pursued his weeping form through the parlor, the library, the pantry, shouting commands at his swift and fleeing back.

When I captured him at last, he wore the expression of an animal smug with unearned fulfillment. His eyes were blister-red, racked with weeping, yet he wept still, wept freely. There was an air of contentment in his weeping that I felt to be incorrect, formally imbalanced, perhaps. Yet when I reached for his throat to amend certain flaws in enunciation, he ceased weeping at once and turned himself away from me. I heard him swallow deeply, as though tucking the remaining sobs into some secret, unseen cavity.

From that moment on, young Victor refused to weep before me, though I often overheard him weeping in private, when lying about in the barn or in some moment of leisure.

5

Victor, I say. Victor, give me your attention. Look at me. I will not ask again.

His great dull head stirs slightly, but remains fixated on a point far to my right. Victor, I say. Victor. Look at me. If you do not look at me, I will have to make use of the rod. I place my hand on the rod for good measure.

He turns his head slowly, achingly toward me. The heavy skull swivels on its stand. It is his chewing-toy that distracts him so, resting naked and exposed upon the side table where I have placed it. He finds it cruel, cruel that he is not permitted to make use of it during this tutorial when I allow it for most of the lectures and dances. I explain again: Victor, we are practicing conversation. We are improving your speech and your pronunciation. You will not improve so long as you insist on keeping that useless bauble in your mouth, where it obscures your breath and proves an obstacle to your tongue, which I remind you has never been as limber as it should.

He seems to have lost interest again. The chewing-toy gleams atop the table, lozenge-shaped and glinting like gold. The rod, I say, remember the rod. With this reminder, he regains a healthy alertness.

Now, Victor, I begin. If another guest should approach you at court and speak to you, uttering the phrase "How do you do?" what should you say?

Victor swivels his tongue around within his mouth, twisting his lips. He has never liked the taste of words, and I sense that he has not developed much of an idea what they are for. He sighs, and his eyes remain upon the toy.

VerywellthankyouandIampleasedtomeetyouhowdoyoudo? he says, all in a rush, his mouth flapping up and down upon the sentence as though it were a piece of meat.

I, myself, am also well, I say. Do you enjoy dancing? I ask.

He stares at me, unsure what to do. I have never given him this prompt before.

Are you enjoying the ball? I ask. This one he has done many times before.

Ohverymuchsowhatareliefitistobeamongpropercompany, he says wearily.

Good, Victor, fairly good, I say. But you would do well to attend to the pauses between your words, for they are as the counts in a measure of music, directing the body toward the greater expression of its own musicality. Measure your breaths, boy, and release them with much care and restraint. Let the words be a dance in themselves, a dance of meaning upon the surface of a tongue.

He stares at me, chewing his finger. He has understood nothing.

6

Swollen-faced Portesquieu leans back in his chair and turns his open maw toward the sky, releasing a moist gibbering of laughter. His mirth strains against the strictures of his clothing, the flesh of his neck bulging sweetly over the stiffened collar. Beads of grease from the lamb leg float upon the dark surface of his ale.

An infant does not learn to discourse on the advantages of walking before it learns to take a step, I declare, assuming a dismissive tone. Rather, the steps teach the walker the value of their use. You would have the infant crawl into old age, if it could not explain why it wished to elevate itself.

And you propose to produce a butterfly by feeding a wolf on rose blossoms and sugar water, Portesquieu replies.

Victor is no wolf, I say. And he shows a tender affection for butterflies and other creatures, one that would shame most well-bred children.

. . .

This tenderness is a topic of conversation among your neighbors, says Portesquieu with an oiled grin. They say your student can be seen from time to time eviscerating small animals on the grounds. Your friend Madame Rameau suffered from strained nerves after witnessing him gnawing with great contentment on the skull of a rabbit, its fur still largely intact. Or perhaps this is a bit of fashionable choreography that I am too dull to comprehend. Were they dancing the gavotte?

He tips the mug down his gullet. The blood pools in my face and I feel flush with sickly warmth. His face before me resembles a pile of meat, arrayed in the shape of a grin.

One needs only to visit my home in the evenings when we practice conversation to observe how beautifully Victor expresses his nature. Come for dinner, and you will see what a sensitive soul might be revealed in any man once you have scraped off the grime, I say, reaching for my mug. I attempt to quaff my ale in a single robust gesture as Portesquieu does, yet it finds a way around my lips and trails down the corner of my mouth, cuts a path across the curvature of my chin.

7

Other villages have had feral children of their own, whom they have reared and educated; they have had wild boys whose unformed minds struggle to grasp the meanings of words and pictures, whose hands grope clumsily at pens. But no other village has had a feral child capable of performing the finest functions of the human body and mind. No other wild-born child has been able to speak with grace and refinement, employing the same terms of politeness and formality as high-born men. No other comports himself like a well-bred boy, or works the flute as nimbly as any middling player. Portesquieu would claim that this is impossible, that a body cultivated in the wild assumes the essence of wildness, turns swampy and will not admit of the growth of more refined habits. But with my labor, I prove him wrong: my wild child dances the minuet on command, as well as several other current dances.

The head must be held upright, but not stiff; the shoulders falling back, extending the breast and giving a greater grace to the body. The arms locked, statuesque, with the left extended down to hip level and the right curving gently in front of the breast, forming a frame around the dancer's body to ornament the proportions of the legs and lend gravity to their movement. Fixing the relations between these parts frees the expressiveness of the lower body, just as the verticality of the human anatomy frees man for complex motions of the hand and intellect. Victor struggles to stay upright as I put him through a series of gentle leaps into each of the five positions. But he is malleable as clay, and his body responds with an eagerness to take form when I correct the placement of his head, feet, and hands, when I press the feared rod to his back in order to demonstrate to him what I mean by "straight, perfectly straight, and upright."

He pants, standing there in fourth position, holding it

decently, but losing shape before my eyes as his body bends beneath the pull of his savagery. At what must be a look of displeasure on my face, I see dismay reflected in his own. Then I go to him and place my hand upon his stunted shoulder, and I say to him that he may leave to have a cry if he likes. I say, Victor. Victor, the work you have been doing is not adequate, but it is admirable. There is no other like you, no other that may demonstrate to the world the civilizing power of art. You are the frozen mammoth, the crocodile. Your presence is proof. Some may hate you for what you bear out, but all will note your ability. To many, you will be a battlefield on which they strive to destroy and slander our accomplishments. But you will always be my garden: a shard of wildness bent into order, a geometric humility carved into the world, and adding to its beauty.

I remove my hand from his shoulder, and he runs off to one of his weeping nooks, I know not which.

8

The body of Victor Tallon reaches the form of its repose: position four, one foot before the other, enabling the smooth transition to a well-practiced bow. The room sings with applause, applause beating against the walls like a hundred clipped birds. Now there is only one dance more that Victor must perform, one dance to prove himself a competent— though not brilliant—executor of the social dances. The lady emerges from the crowd, a young girl close to Victor's age, the age experts imagine him to be. This is the courante, a couple's dance, and a dance of such exquisite tenderness and modesty that it is certain to stir the emotions of the audience. The two partners shall approach one another from opposite ends of the floor, facing each other briefly as mirror images of masculine and feminine grace, before turning toward the front to commence the inscription of delicately wrought arcs and turns invisibly upon the ballroom floor: mirroring each other yet never touching, like the sun and the moon drawing twin circles around our days.

Victor and the young lady approach each other tentatively. Her face wears a sweetly youthful air, set within a complexion of lilies and purified milk—though I notice also a tinge of trepidation. His face is at first a bit difficult to glimpse through the elaborate costumes of my fellow onlookers, but I move left and right until I see him clearly. His face holds an expression that I cannot recall having seen before: a smile, a true smile spreads over his face as he nears her, a true upward lifting of the edges of the lips such as I have never witnessed. He gazes at her like one waking from a sleep that has lasted a lifetime. It is as I imagined: the noble spirit that imbues the dances of our age have awakened a noble sensibility in my savage boy. He lives, he moves, he loves! My heart heaves in my chest, an organ sighing with well-deserved peace. The girl's face smiles in response, but her troubled demeanor increases visibly.

I look to Victor. His smile has grown since I last observed it: now it reveals teeth, and a bit of fine, healthy gum. I look to the girl, her eyes clogged with fear. Victor's gaze rests upon her décolletage, fixed to a point beneath which her heart beats hot, quick, like a rabbit's. Victor, I say. Then I notice the young girl's necklace.

Delicate, finely made, and strung with several lozenges of

real gold, gleaming like teeth in the candlelit room. Victor, I say. There is a resemblance, I say, but those are not yours at all, not yours to chew, they are not the same thing at all. The room is still, and I do not know whether I speak these words aloud, or utter them only in the pit of my stomach.

Victor bears on with an expression of unutterable joy. His mouth plunges forward, open and full of hard white points. I feel like weeping. With my hands I grope at invisible strings, which do not exist. I look to Portesquieu, but he looks straight ahead, his pillowy face tightening. I turn my head and stare out the casement window at the royal gardens instead, wet and slippery and dark as the center of a body, where the roses twitch an extinguished red.

A Brief History of Weather

IN SNOW

When a father returns to empty shelves, empty cupboards, and a family that can only sit there, parched, playing one of many games centered around counting to larger and ever larger numbers, he will retrieve the luggage that he has brought back with him, bring the brown suitcase, the suitcase with two brass latches, opening it up before our eyes to reveal that it is full of snow.

Before our eyes he opens it up, his hands slip back the two latches in clean sound, and then the snow seen against a silk lining, paisley-printed, all the snow glaring back the lamps and shaming our house with the brilliance of things that belong outside it.

The snow is what sand would be if it could forget its material, if it could forget its hardness, roughness, if it could forget its own weight. And the snow is what we would be if we could forget ours. If we could become the things we pretend instead of merely pretending at them, playing over and over at a game of falling silent and soft from couch to floor, making ourselves silent and soft as we can, playing at being snow, playing until our elbows and sides are too sore to move.

Before our eyes he makes small motions at the contents of the suitcase, and the snow begins to fill out, piling the table and over the table to the floor. Then we are in up to our knees.

WE ARE THE WEATHER

The weather is beautiful through the windows of our house, you could take it for a painting. With an ear pressed to the window, it speaks, stutters, moist noises like someone in a form of forced sleep.

Right now it rains. Water throws itself against our windows, sideways with the force of the wind. It makes the things outside melt, dripping off gelatinous blots of their own color. How wonderful to be able to melt the shape from things that belong so smugly to themselves. To be the outside itself, or to reach for it and feel something without the flat touch of glass.

Father proclaims man and weather natural enemies, and suddenly we are. In motion his mouth laps at the air, takes into it the world we have been presented with and passes it out again, deformed. Pressed against tongue, teeth, the sounds fall out marked by indentations from human molars. They take shapes that imply our own deformation, that cause us to turn over the words in our own mouths, heavy and cold like a mouthful of marbles that taste of the hands of other children.

Father names the body of man a device for sculpting weather more weatherlike, less crazed, a device for disciplining the air. He walks out into the daylight shaking damaged equipment toward the mild sky. As hollow tubes spill from his arms, as springs jerk wildly, taut and loose, flinging themselves like a ruined cartoon body, knotted together and dancing. His voice going on without punctuation without pause about the ruined possibilities of his invention, his

invention a device intended to transform one thing into another, that takes it away from itself and makes it one's own,
as my father to the weather or my mother to her projects of
paper and thread. In the partial daylight, a father fills up
with shadow, standing as a silhouette of a machine shuddering up and down as it works, wobbly, clanking against itself,
a machine for the production of heat and noise.

My father, certain that internal forms of weather can be
used to influence the external. My father under the big sky,
shouting at clouds. We watch him through a window. We
play rain, rubbing our hands and faces all over the smooth
surfaces of the furniture.

MEASURED FACTS

We have invented a meter to measure the accumulation of time, a machine capable of producing detailed descriptions of the air. We have invented a method of extracting still water from rain and for shaming sleet and slush into legible forms of precipitation, forms a child could draw.

The surface of our home is a single block of shatterproof plastic. There is a single flaw in the surface of our home through which we would enter or exit, a thing we rarely do.

Air enters the flaw of a body and presses through into ever-deeper regions, traveling from oral reservoir to tracheal passageway to the lungs, which resemble small rooms. This is illustrated in a diagram fixed to the dining room wall, which is designed to remind us to keep food and air passages separate. In this diagram, a frog sits in a glass-sided tank. The frog is a cross-section, and air is a blue arrow traveling into its body. In the diagram to its right, the arrow is red, and represents food traveling the same path to the lungs. I point to this second frog, which is dead.

"Many thousands of years ago, the world's surface was covered with small, thoughtless beings whose deaths held no consequences. In the terrible storms of lava and rain that occurred before the climate had come to a form of sense, they died and multiplied like a storm in themselves, flourishing haphazardly and then collapsing into a pit or whatnot where their lungs filled with the syrupy weight of their own liquefied ancestors. They lived like the weather, like a smattering of problems unforeseen but urgent, and they died, too, like the showers or sunlight: a brief seizure with no purpose, no understanding of their own duration."

A necessary flaw belongs somewhere between an error and a mistake.

Our device to control the weather fails to control anything at all.

DREAMING WATER

We play a game based upon the weather, it begins in the living room. We stand in the middle, looking around. One player will ask, "Do you think it's going to rain?" and the other will answer. I hold out my hand.

"I think I feel some drops, just a few."

Look up at the ceiling, search it for clouds.
Describe the color of the clouds and their shape.
This one like a duck, that one like an anvil.

Demonstrate surprise.

Cirrus clouds indicate cold weather if they move from left to right. Cumulus clouds indicate rain if they are gray, stacked, or have grown taller throughout the day. Stratus clouds can bring snow flurries or storm. A cloud shaped like an anvil impends.

Describe the direction of their movement. Describe their speed.
I open an imaginary newspaper.
    The newspaper opens like wings, makes their sound.
    Gray squares tremble against the air.

    "It says there's a thirty percent chance."

We watch the ceilings, and the minutes remove themselves.

TO UNDO OR NOT TO DO

This device is a vaporizer. It is for clouds, sunshine, temperature, and wind. It is also for plants and other living things.

When I say it is for them, I do not mean that it is good for them.

This device is heavier than almost anything. It has a case made of metal stuck through with tubes leading from one place within it to another. No matter how hard you lean against it, it does not sway. No matter how hard you kick it, it does not respond to or do anything. Under no circumstances is it to be kicked or pushed.

When the rain falls, bit by bit it becomes broken. I watch the rain falling on it, falling on its body and its back, falling into the funnel from which it acts out, falling all over it so it makes a sound like a thousand drums and I know suddenly that as heavy as it is, it is hollow past the shell. All is different kinds of gray. It gives off small stars as the rain knits it in water.

What our family has done, the rain undoes in a matter of minutes. The color of the sky and the ground, it undoes. Undone, the dryness and smooth feeling of the air. If it could undo also the year or two years that have come before, would we be as we were, or would we be something new, wetter?

. . .

I hold my ruined pet, looking out the window at the rain, the rain, the substance that would either bring my pet back, or turn it into something more distant, untouchable.

PLAY HOUSE

Outdoors, water soaks the ground and is lost. Indoors we live with rules that prevent things from becoming lost or broken, from leaking outdoors and coming loose.

These are obstructions that redirect absences before they unfold, closed spaces in which things are not forced to pass out of view in time like everything else, like a sudden dissipation replacing the light with its hollow or the objects of the day with their opposites, a flower with its absence or the shape of a pet with a thin, tasteless vapor. We pass these things from our view instead with willed movements away, we leave them by force and when we return to them in several minutes or hours or days, they remain.

In this way, our house resembles a life tied in a knot, or a passage of time spread out in all directions. There are long spaces unfilled by anything, then sudden clumps of familiar and unfamiliar strewn as in a salvage yard, portions that have "stepped to the side, safe, rather than eliminating themselves violently." Indoors we may construct our lives from tissue paper, from brittle thread, from confectioner's sugar, if we wish. Materials that crumble at the touch or sag under moisture live like magazine images beneath our ceilings, they will not wish to stir within our thick walls, repaired constantly with special tools we have made to preserve their form. We might be anyone, and our undoing just another thing rolling around like a marble through the halls, waiting to be found and left and lost and forgotten.

. . .

My mother sits, making small scratching motions with the fingers to coax the meanings from flat objects. I run from the room. I run back into the room. I run from the room and make small scratching motions at the wall, yielding little. I run through the house. I search my father, to go to him for the words to fill these descriptions. He stands in front of the window, practicing his speech. I run from the room. I run back into the room. These are the things we make possible in an environment salvaged from its own predisposition toward destruction.

NEVER HAVE I EVER

I lie in the center of the emptiest room of our emptiest house looking from right to left. The room breathes around me as I lie more like a floor than the flattest, deadest floor. Looking down over the belly, I see the sockets and lights rise up and down, up and down steadily, and I can make it breathe more quickly by breathing more quickly, until I feel dizzy and my head rolls over in circles.

We study the weather from within this house, and we are the weather within this house. Outside this house there are weather and weather patterns, stretching for miles in any direction. We cannot control the weather from within this house. But in this house we are working on it.

We study the weather in a house that keeps the weather out, we watch the weather outdoors from indoors, through the windows. We can see rain through the windows, sleet through the windows, hail, snow, partially cloudy, cloudy with a chance of thunderstorms, partially cloudy with isolated thunderstorms. We can see fog through the windows, but we cannot see what lies past it.

Indoors we have cataloged the indoors, named its parts and recorded their number and location. We remove their ability to surprise us, even as they relieve us of our astonishment. It seems as though this indoors is held up by these numbers: if they were to become lost, it would vanish like pots and pans when one forgets they are playing house.

. . .

Weather covers the length of a wooden fence. It covers over our backyard and the backyards of our neighbors, who have all disappeared. Where did they disappear to, and how?

They disappeared like weather, like weather the day after weather.

UNTIL SOMETHING HAPPENS

We approach the cold like the water approaches the bottom of a hill. It makes itself felt through the holes in our airtight windows, six inches of solid plastic. He rolled everyone in thick acrylic fleece, I saw nothing but white and a small circle of mixed color. We roasted and ate large wheels of meat, meat being "the command given to another body, setting it in purposeful motion with knives and grinding." There was nothing to do and there was less of it every day, the husks of board games drained in the corner of every room, their only use brief and saddening. Pick it up, look for something new to appear printed on the reverse side, try to use the game pieces on another board, grow heavy, carry to another room and leave in that corner, a new corner. The winter "like an abomination paralleled only by the flaccidity of spirit with which it has been met with in response." The winter "the gravest threat to productive and life-affirming activity to enter these walls since the homequake of three autumns prior," but making a sound more like that of mice inching under the floorboards or of fire scratching at the outer shell. One night, they read and I look at pictures in a large atlas of other places to be. On other nights, I read and Father argues about great inventions of the past. Or we listen to forecasts over the radio.

The first idea was a house without weather, says Father. The same idea as a roof, but bigger. Better, he says. Mother looks up from her work. She is making a blue scarf out of woolen yarn, another blue scarf to add to the piles of blue scarves, hats, mittens, muffs that sit over there in the closet, getting older.

PERCENTAGE OF CLEAR SKY

Of the types and the shapes. Of arranging them in groups by height, weight, or self-similarity. Of the types of children they once were and could someday give birth to. Other people and their ability to pass freely through the space that you take up, to pass to and through and away from it in a way that you were not designed to do.

Once upon a time other people were around. You could see them through the window. They were washing their minivans, vacuuming debris up from under the car mats. They were playing with a dog, or tousling its ears, or scratching the scruff of its neck under the collar. You could see from their faces that they loved soccer, or horses, or mornings. They had preferences for large things over small, or the opposite.

What happened inside their houses, besides a choreography of lights going on and off and, eventually, entirely off?

How did they know when to turn which lights on and off, and to what end?

Distance and knowledge are nearly the same thing. Or so my family tells me, demonstrating this by covering my eyes with small pieces of white paper and asking me to identify what I see. Children have been visible outside the window, playing in the snow as though unaware of its crystalline structure, each one fragile and irreproducible. I have watched the snow melt in their hands, though I have not felt it melt in my own.

ONLY SLIGHTLY

My mother watches the storm from the kitchen window of this house, watches the storm fall over roof and yard. It falls from the sky through a fiberglass frame of approximately a foot in diameter, suspended outside the kitchen window by a hermetically sealed plastic pipe, the pipe's opening governed by vacuum pump, ending in an airtight seal.

When it rains good, clean rain, when it rains types of rain that we have not encountered previously, or familiar types that can replenish our collections. Then we will make it sleep, we will put it under ether.

I watch her at the window, loading a canister of gaseous substance, checking air pressure within canister and pipe, preparing the pump for operation and checking its parts for leakage and wear. At the peak of the storm, when the sounds of individual raindrops falling upon the roof are no longer distinguishable one from the other, she presses the button and the frame fills with mist.

My mother dons raincoat, gloves, galoshes, and an oversize hat. She opens the umbrella and steps outside, gingerly over the cobblestones, gingerly to the collection tank. The plastic frame is filled with droplets of water suspended in midair, shaped like downward momentum, but paused there. Paused. She takes the large glass jar from beneath her coat and fills it with sleeping rain. The cap again atop the jar.

We have learned that the weather cannot be kept outdoors and must be brought indoors, dragged indoors, before it brings itself indoors. We create the image of a house where the outside must ask to be let in, where it rings the bell and wonders what to do with its hands while it waits for someone to come to the door. Through such preemptive tactics we show it that, though it may cover the whole world, we cover the world inside our house.

When my mother comes back, she leaves the jar on the kitchen counter. The raindrops inside look sad or exhausted. They stir, but only slightly.

LEARNED MOTIONS

We maintain a constant temperature of 73 degrees within our house, counteracting temperature drops with baths and warm foods, counteracting rises in temperature with meals of ice and cold water.

We gather in photographs in triangular formations, the hands of the two larger on the shoulders of the smaller, as if we could become a single solid structure.

Nineteenth-century physicist Arthur Worthington photographed drops of milk at their moment of impact with a hard surface, providing irrefutable evidence of "the deeply lodged gimpishness of nature at her core." While scientists had previously imagined the splash patterns of liquids to be regular, symmetrical, crystalline, the photographs taken within Worthington's laboratory revealed ragged blooms that threw themselves up into the air with "indiscrimination worthy only of a pratfall." They surged up upon impact, or seemed to reach outward with irregularly sized pseudopodia. With this material proof of their irregularity, naturally occurring phenomena entered the category of "trainable effects," like "the squelching and spattering sounds that emerge from a mouth in the process of doing other than generating meaningful speech" that we silence with practice and much cloth.

The walls of our house are to its space as the rules are to a game. In between lie air, and everything allowed. We run

circles from the kitchen through the den through the bed-
rooms through the kitchen.

Controlling the weather will be the first step past building
descriptions that cannot hold it in. It could be the first step
out of this house that we have lived so far into and through.

MANY QUESTIONS

At dusk, we play a game of thought and guessing. This is recreation, which fills the spaces between moments of productive friction, moments in which we create. In the dusk, the space within takes on a color to which it is difficult to respond. We want to turn the lights on but it is too early, we want to keep them off but it grows too late. We want a space in which we could half do, do halfway, but we are forced to be one thing or another, except within the act of hoping.

Our family, like other collections, possesses a nested structure. My father has known the most and thus could know us better than we know ourselves: he could dream us and we would not know the difference. My mother has seen less and knows proportionately less, and I know the least possible. I could fold up into her, and her into him. We would live inside him like a house, one large white house with two tiny windows on the front. In this house we would have all the things we have now, but we would have no father.

The game is called Many Questions. It happens like this:

I'm thinking of an object, my father says.

Is it a refrigerator? asks my mother.

No, it is not, he replies.

Is it my kitten? I ask.

No, no, he answers.

Is it a stop sign? asks my mother.

It is not, he replies. Now, why in the world would I think of that?

THAT WHICH MEETS NO RESISTANCE

The first idea was to build a house free of weather. Mother says Father was sleepless for weeks, drawing plans for houses without doors, without windows, houses without pipes for outdoor water to enter, houses without any air inside at all.

The first idea was to build a house free of weather. But they discovered within the removal processes a second-ary origin of weather. A house with nothing to resist—no rain, no wind—finds areas of resistance within, growing frustrated with its own stasis, shuddering and crumbling around its own stable shape. He formulated a rule: *The shelter that meets no resistance shall resist itself.*

It was many days ago that Father's rule was proven accu-rate and, conversely, that our house proved itself to be a rule. I curled around my warmth as the morning opened itself up, peacefully, without even drops of dew or the movement of birds outdoors. A sharp whine began from within the walls and floor, making items of furniture whine too, like a bomb about to go off. The things on the walls fell off during this whining, and the things on the tables fell with the onset of a chugging, painful sound from machines somewhere within the house. Around us, two gulps softly and one spasm like an attempt to hurl something from the throat. I said that it seemed the house felt we were alien, but I was told that was unlikely. The machinery, built to withstand high winds and violent events, was simply buckling under the weight of very little: through induced outer turbulence we would regain the internal stillness that comforted our objects and our routines. The floor was on a tilt and I watched the round things roll away and out of the room, and the flat and square things slide more slowly toward a similar exit. In another room the refrigerator was on fire, burning up from inside, smelling at once like charred meat and plastic.

I open the freezer door and stare at the hail. It stays still in there. It looks back at me from next to the ice cream and some frozen peas, the hailstones beginning to stick to the freezer's artificial frost.

THE FIRST IDEA

From one room I looked for another room to hold me, to change the things around me and leave this sharp feeling behind me in the sharp air. A feeling might claw you open with the simple intention of freeing itself, and it would be no one's fault. I took the black marker from the top of the table.

One arrives at the map room, taking long steps through the shuddering hall. Charts of yesterday's weather and to-day's weather and tomorrow's weather cover the walls and windows. This is where we make the fiction of tomorrow's weather, which we hope to make fact, where we draw the weather on the maps, draw the future on their flat faces.

I drew storms on the maps of yesterday and today.

There had been no storms yesterday or today.

The world of the future will be "storm-free, an environment designed for utter compatibility with the needs of the many, as determined through a survey reconstructing the median desires of a high-quality section of inhabitants." It will wheeze rather than roar. Instead of the storm, there will be a pocket of mild, warm wind. Instead of the rain there will be light and additional light, filling every corner of the empty sky. Instead of hiding from it as one, we will scatter, walking aimlessly away from a central point to a peripheral.

. . .

I drew a storm with a warm front traveling north toward this house, a low-pressure center. I marked the origin of storm activity and the counterclockwise direction of wind flow around the low-pressure center.

LACK OF WIND

The clouds we make with the breathing machine are too heavy, and will not float in the air. For now, we strap a harness to them and hang them from the rafters, but we will run out of room, even in this house designed to substitute the sky.

A small, simple game played using words printed on white note cards, and a small black-and-white board. Mother takes a card from the top of the deck and reads it out:

Move back three spaces.

It is my turn, and I move the piece that stands for me three spaces backward on the board. Tiny, useless clouds roll by like tumbleweeds. Or would, if any wind blew within the walls of our house.

I look toward my sister.

It is Father's turn and I read it out:

Move back one space.

Father moves his piece back one space, and takes the first card off the top of the pile:

Move back two spaces.

Mother moves her piece back two spaces. She takes the next card from the top of the pile. But I take myself to the map room, where I draw angry storms all across the midwestern United States, and both coasts.

A SMALL, SIMPLE GAME

I wander us to the room where clouds are constructed, and now we sisters look upon the same machines with similar eyes. Surrounding us are the freezing chambers, the artificial breathers, the cloud-molds and cloud-cutters.

The first of our homemade clouds were made of real breath, sighed and heaved into the chambers through an air tube. These clouds were perfect and small and a child could name them, pretending that they were a pet cat or dog. These clouds achieved a maximum volume of 6.5 liters, the vital capacity of my father's lungs.

But larger clouds were required to replicate natural weather, and the artificial breathers were therefore invented to be larger than us, and better than us at accomplishing things they did not even want to accomplish. Like a huge plastic tube, a huge rubber lung, the mechanical breathers breathed all through the night, wheezing through dream after dream, collapsing themselves into flat rubber sacks and then drawing back up, well-oiled and smooth, and filling the chambers with a strange, moist breath that congealed into weird uncloudlike shapes.

To achieve standardized clouds for my mother's experiments, we took these clouds that felt a little wooly, a little wet, and pushed them into the molds, making the shapes of cumulus, nimbus, cirrus, stratus, fog.

The day the machine broke, there was barely a real cloud in the sky. The blue stretched pale and cool over my father, arms full of machine scrap jostling as he strode around in sharp patterns like a ball striking against invisible obstacles, emitting liters of shouting. The blue opened up over layers and layers of empty space waiting to be filled up with big soft shapes that we had chosen. It gaped above as, at the end of the driveway, no longer shouting, he crumpled downward.

INSTEAD OF ONE

My sister is either older than me or younger than me.

She is either better than me or she is less good.

Under the right circumstances, she is able to put aside self-doubt and leap into action with reflexes that harken back to a more instinctual time, rescuing the child from the onslaught of truck wheels, train wheels, car wheels, saving the child's life and earning the respect of townspeople and journalists.

Or else she is unable to.

The utility of a sister stems from the longing for reinforcement, for an additional, aligned person inside the house to see what is happening and feel some way about it.

This has something to do with why we are fitted with two eyes instead of one.

WE HAVE DREAMED FOR THEM

Approximately the same height, almost certainly the same age, we sisters crawl hand and knee down a sidewalk we have imagined to exist: three feet wide, five hundred feet long, sidling past a series of miniature houses lined up like the silences in a single day. Preferring one and then the other, we invest in these houses one by one as though we were able to see only halfway through them, through the front facade in a cutaway view, and not all the way.

In the living room, at half size, in the transparent homes we have dreamed for them and placed in our own, we crawl on hands and knees to peer in at one and the next. We have made them of ice and they melt, but slowly. The object of the game is to resist seeing all the way through these glass walls to the familiar objects that lie beyond them, to the old armchair with a dun doily on each tattered arm. Mothers and fathers in these homes of glass turn toward us and smile small, shining, glass smiles, holding up their smiles and their hands in greeting, standing still among perfect stacks of sandwiches: white bread, peanut butter, bananas. This mother, whistling as she fills brown paper bags. That mother, waving at us with one arm, the other arm around the shoulders of a gigantic glass of milk.

At this, my sister stops suddenly and makes a motion as if to dive in and leave us separate, lonesome. I grab the back of her dress and hold tight but she is so hard to hold still, my hands finding no place to make of her a handle or a knot. She whines low and mournfully, signaling as though she would like to crawl inside. Small, silly sister. She has not seen that the spell of play lasts only so long as one pretends not to wish to grasp the things that we have played into being.

In one house, they make snowman versions of themselves, which come slowly to life and begin slowly a series of ordinary things that the family watches, entranced. The snowmen notice us watching, then all the inhabitants of the house turn to us and wave.

In another house, they invent a device to control the weather. When I look into this house and count the number of persons inside, I begin to cry.

WITH TWO

The fact of two sisters allows an escape into situations that could not be accommodated by only one. With two, we may hide in the cupboard for hours, pretending we are somewhere else entirely, without ever having to feel ourselves alone.

From the cupboard, I gaze at her and beckon her in. My knees hunched up by my ears.

The fact of two sisters allows for escape within a situation that is hostile or unfair. Certain species of cicadas lie dormant in their burrows for seventeen years of hibernation, before bursting forth to eat and eat and fly about in the air.

Certain species of birds time their own hatching to meet the soft new cicadas when they emerge.

I set the table, four plates and four sets of silverware for our small careful family.

With her face set in a shape of preoccupation, my mother removes the fourth plate and places it back in the cupboard.

I see my sister's face grinning back at me from the cupboard, a space so small I cannot imagine how I would fit with her in there.

EACH ONE LIKE THE NEXT

I can see my sister crouching in the living room, playing over something I cannot see.

A toy?

The reasons for a sister are manifold, and if we could persuade her to speak she would give them for herself. The house is emptier every day, less populated, the doors all shut, the objects seem to disappear from tabletops. It is like a leak has opened up someplace we cannot see or sense; there has been no one to watch or be watched by. The eyes grow restless, finding faces in the folds of curtains, crockery, closets.

For another, too few games can be played alone.

I played a game alongside my parents at breakfast. It began with all players picking up a section of the newspaper and opening it up at the fold. My father shakes it three or four times, with a disappointed sound. My mother begins with the headlines and then the little sections, then the longer articles. We went through it, piece by piece, until all was read. We consumed the little letters in their little blocks, then we turned the page for the others.

My newspaper was imaginary, and I finished first.

I watch from the doorway, an empty frame. This door has been taken off its hinges to prevent it from being slammed shut. The resulting air flow, expelled at the velocity of anger, could shake a house to dust. The door has been taken off and taken where?

UNHABITED

A house at night should not be woken into alone, if other methods can be made available. The presence of a parent via effigy, by means of photograph or even an object that they have been seen to love, hate, or merely hold, may be presented to the darkened house as evidence of the presence, past or future, of others with an investment in your existence. The notion of a linkage between yourself and another, by means of structure or form, will impress the house and render it less likely to target you with unidentified sounds and shadows.

We play a game involving the description of the walls, but we are both so good at it that we cannot but fail to surprise each other.

Are there ghosts in the house, and if there were, how would they have gotten in? I tuck the quilt in under my feet, I close the closet door and turn on three different nightlights. These things will yield, if not safety, then an allusion to the idea of it. If there were ghosts in the house, how lonely would they be? With no one to see me, I become like a vapor.

The emptiness within the house populates what lies beyond it. Lightning walks the plain like a tall, glowing man. He looks toward me and at once he is gone.

WE COULD DO IT ALONE

I explain to her the mechanics of daring. She must step outside the door. Outside the door, the day roils with temperatures that would touch our skin.

I explain it. Gameplay proceeds by turns, with each player advancing the series by one. One player's proposal for action on the part of another is balanced by a counterproposal for a different sort of action by a different person. She must step outside the door. But when will the action be performed? The emphasis is upon daring, not doing. If it were only about doing, we could do it alone, in our separate rooms, with the door closed. I explain to her that this process may bring joy nevertheless, though she remains impermeable to this point, sprawled sideways on the carpet and staring deeply into it.

As I watch her stare under the couch or into the cabinets, I imagine that she may be dissatisfied with the network of beings and objects that she is required to live among. Escape from the scale she was born into could be achieved by burrowing into phenomena of a different scale, belonging to the world of much larger or smaller things.

Our father, for example, has escaped us, has escaped deeper into the house or laboratory, to a position behind a final door through which the sounds of shouting are audible. Our mother proceeds laterally, walking her eyes around at their much greater height, as if in a walking form of sleep. They exist for their work, and are lost to us now.

Experienced by a much smaller being, this day would glow with the excess beauty of certain of its shorter intervals. The moment, for example, when a spoon fell from the table and onto the kitchen floor in the brilliance of an un-lonely afternoon. Stretched to a beautiful length, the resulting sound would have rung out for nearly an hour, rung out like a force of nature, a piece of the air. We would not have had to think of a new game, living our joys in the shadow of this long, loud sound.

Even with all this in mind, she must step outside the door.

I AM LIKE I AM NOT THERE

Standing before the door, I speak to her. I explain to her the ultimate aim of the game of daring: to dare someone to do what is impossible to do, and thereby undo themselves. With this in mind, I dare her to open the door and step through it. Into the murderous gales of the sky, I say, though I cannot see the sky from in here. She looks at me glassy-eyed. She has become more doll-like day by day, spending her hours heaped sideways and still, looking under the furniture at things I can only infer. I repeat myself and wait for surrender.

My sister looks toward the door and places one small hand on the lock. I hear a small, clean turning sound and the rush of air. Then she is over the threshold and moving. I run to the door to close the air out. But I open it again slightly, I watch her through the gap in the door.

Both arms out straight and extended, she walks like someone on a balance beam, down the driveway, teetering away from the door, away from me, twirling around, hopping on an imaginary hopscotch grid. The sunlight draws a yellow haze around her, her hair, her small false hands. Watching her walk away is like watching myself depart, though when I look down, I find I am in place.

At the end of the driveway, she turns and looks back at me from a distance.

Then she is gone.

YOUR MOVE

I plunge my whole fist into the jam jar. I write my name, and your name, all your names, on the wall. I tidy the china with a soft dustcloth. I rage and rage and rage and rage at the furniture that still resembles human beings, at the ones shaped like people I shout my language. There seem to be fewer. I am picking the blueberries out of the muffins, the toppings off the frozen pizzas, still frozen. Ever ever fewer. I am shiny, sticky. I run around and around, trailing berry-colored handprints, and when I get back to the start I grow silent and track myself, quietly, through the halls, soundlessly, I am like I am not there, I am there like I am not there, I am my own ghost trailing my own ghost to some indeterminate point in time, forward and backward on a track made of iron. I plunge my fist into the jam jar. I make a peanut butter and jelly sandwich of the fatherly armchair. Where have you all gone? So I write your name on the sticky surface. So I dust the furniture, even lifting the vases, plates, etcetera, to clean under them. But no one is pleased. No one is bothered. There is no one to be pleased. I rule these lands, and there are none that could dare question these acts, or declare them unjust, or affirm that they have come to pass or have not. As a result, do they come undone? I try to do a thing so large or heavy that it recognizes itself, that it does not need someone else to see it to make it endure. I try to carve my name into the wall. I tie all the things to one another with red string. It will not guard against their leaking, slowly, from inside these walls and out, who knows.

FACTS LIKE FACES

I play a game of making it rain. I fill the sky with clouds, I label and describe them one by one. They are all different types, collecting at the ceiling of the living room. I check the forecast in the newspaper, I comment on the dark storm brewing overhead. I hold my hand out, but I feel nothing.

It is necessary that "the child find him or herself confronted by his or her own increasingly 'ordered' behavior as, from the world of practice and play, the world of the adult is grown into." Is it necessary for this world to be so quiet, its contents captured between parentheses?

When the actual shape of the liquid's breakage was discovered, there were two basic tactics that could have been adopted. The first was to reshape the preferences of the liquid, training it toward a manageable complexity that would reveal itself legibly—as a hexagon or a torus, for example. The second would have been to reshape ourselves.

In the context of the development of an organism into an organism that masters its surroundings, reshaping ourselves would have been to "grow backward."

Backward was the more populated direction, and had a tendency to look beautiful as a result. The orientation of our faces on the fore side of our bodies, luckily, made it more difficult to see and long for that direction, which was becoming farther away all the time.

OUT OF DOORS

I wake to a Mother standing by the bed, a Father by the window with his hand on the cord, pulling the blinds open. The blinds are never open.

The sky outside is strange, its papery surface, its white flank. Be handed a coat, a hat, a set of galoshes. We are going outdoors. We never go outdoors.

We have one driveway and it is never used. It leads from the garage with its one shiny car, down past our door, past a little path that leads from our door, past our door, down to a mailbox that we have not looked inside for quite some time.

Mother on one side, Father on the other, a family walks down the driveway to the end of the driveway. It is as though we have never used our eyes before, we are looking right and left, right and left.

Today is a day without weather. We don't know where it went, but it has gone and thus we walk around, soft-skinned, into the air. Is this walking the ultimate aim of my Father's efforts to cancel the weather? Are we achieved at last?

There is no wind, there is no water. There is light. There is no sense that something in the sky will heave or change color. The only air that moves is air we push from our lungs.

II.

I May Not Be the One You Want,
But I Am the One for You

Karen watched him waiting, standing, shifting in place at the counter and sliding his pale dry hands in and out of his pockets. The coffee shop was noisy, but she could still hear the hands as they burrowed into their stiff cavities, making a sound like safety razors scraped across a leg. She could hear something about this man's life in that sound, or she thought she could hear it—that was the only way to explain why she was beginning to dislike him even though he had done nothing to her, said nothing to her at all. She imagined his chapped hands caressing the stubble on his own face, she imagined his fear of speaking in public or giving a presentation. A small, rubbery tongue twisting within the dry mouth. Karen hadn't been near people for some weeks, and now when they were around their presence was almost unbearably sensual. He looked toward her and smiled stiffly. He had a compact and tightly formed skull.

Karen looked back at her computer reflexively. She was working on an article about a dairy farmer in northern New Jersey. The article was three weeks late. To her left, a young woman with streaky blond hair pasted a cover letter from one Internet browser window into another. A man hunched over a small laptop erased the nipple from a photo of a woman. Karen had signed on to do the article last summer, when she was living in a different apartment and still had a boyfriend. The article was a slam dunk, a home run, as her friend Vanessa had put it drunkenly the other night. It profiled a man who others in the business of rearing dairy cattle referred to as the "Holstein Einstein." Ned Regan was the epitome of a caring, humane dairy farmer, one who could make you feel good again about using the bodies of animals. His small herd of about 150 hormone-free, antibiotic-free milk cows had names and nicknames, family trees drawn up by hand and tucked away in Ned's old khaki green filing cabinets, and homeopathic dandelion compresses applied to their engorged nipples to soothe sore udders. Ned's competitors spoke of him with reverence: his cows gave the most milk and this milk, like a fine wine, had notes of cherry and smooth oak. Karen had been doing fairly well at the Regan farm up until the last few days. Since she had been back she worked only when it was dark outside, writing for ten minutes at a time and then napping out the rest of the hour. She went out only after midnight to buy a meatball sandwich at the corner deli. She had written eighteen different first paragraphs.

Now there was nobody waiting at the counter. She looked around her at dozens of bodies spaced one foot, two feet apart. Then she noticed him there, in the rightmost seat, holding an unopened bottle of water out toward her.

"This is for you," he said.

Karen looked at it. It was beautiful water, the sort she didn't buy.

"I saw you were empty," he said.

He indicated a little plastic cup on her table. To her left, someone released a loud sputtering laugh at a vigorously animated figure on their computer screen.

"It's good," he added, nodding.

She reached out slowly and took it in her hands. The bottle of water was a tiny diorama, heavy and plastic-cool. Clear, pure water tipped back and forth across a tiny photo of a tropical landscape. In the foreground, a little waterfall plunged from the top of a mossy cliff into a deep, refreshing lagoon the color of toothpaste. The tropical water was festooned with little white glints of sunshine, small sharp waves. She looked into the distance at the miniature mountains, shrouded in pixelated mist. But where were all the fish, the birds, the vacationing tourists with their bikinis and cameras? They've all drowned, Karen realized suddenly. She put the bottle down.

"Thank you," she said.

The man smiled again, his little mouth smooth and slightly pink. She felt bad for having disliked him while he was standing up there at the counter, buying water for her. She thought of buying him something. Saying something pleasant to him. She felt thick-brained and inept at the delicate choreography of being nice to people. She had been watching two movies a day, sometimes more. There were almost enough movies around to live your entire life in them. But there were not quite enough. Last night she had watched all six installments of a miniseries about espionage during the Cold War. In this series, people were terrible and the protagonist was boring. The plot centered on finding out who within the bureau was a double agent, and though there was ultimately only one double agent many of the main character's friends betrayed him in small, inconsequential ways. When at last the protagonist returned to the orderly apartment where he lived alone, alone despite having resolved a major national crisis, Karen felt so angry, without reason or direction, that she cried in the loud way, the way that sounds like choking.

"This water looks great," said Karen. She nudged it on the table, but did not pick it up. She smiled tightly. "It's nice," she said, feeling like she hadn't said enough. "It's pretty."

"My name is Martin," said the man solemnly.

"I'm Karen," said Karen.

"I'm working," she explained.

"Yes," said Martin. "So am I. I'm sorry to disturb you."

He had a slight accent, his words were blurry. He wore a blazer and a red and black striped T-shirt with a small, useless pocket sewn onto it. He was fairly attractive, with a face like an exsanguinated Jared Leto. While Martin turned back to his computer, Karen listened to the sound of his breath, even and calming, a foot and a half away.

Karen still hadn't settled on a title for the article, and she stared again at the list of phrases she had been able to come up with. At Home On the Range. The Holstein Whisperer. Some were just phrases: Milk-Fed, Whole Milk, The Milky Way. She opened the document up and tried to start again, this time beginning with her arrival at Ned Regan's dairy farm. The gentle green hills. The round smell of cow manure, the soft sounds of grass tearing and flat teeth chewing ambiently everywhere. She and Tim had broken up the week before she went to stay at the farm; was that important? Would it add something? Ned Regan's hard jaw, handsome but set at an unhandsome angle, like it was sliding off the side of his face. And the cows, all the cows, their hipbones jutting up, moving past her at almost eye level. Once they were too old to produce milk, they would be eaten. Martin was bent over his keyboard, his back supple, while he scrolled down, down, continuously down, stroking the trackpad with one finger. He looked utterly absorbed. A feeling of loneliness overtook her. "What are you working on?" she asked, and tried to lean a little toward him. Karen's ex-boyfriend Tim hadn't written or called in over four days, even though he had said that he would check up on her once she got back to the city.

"I am re-creating a website," said Martin, sitting up and blinking at her with his round, factual eyes. "It is an artist's website, a photographer. I create the infrastructure," he said, drawing something like a box in the air with thin fingers.

"I am from Germany," he said.

"Oh," said Karen. "That's interesting."

"I am here for work," said Martin. "I am staying in the neighborhood, with a friend. We work together on this project. We had a great deal to do."

"I'm writing an article," said Karen. "Beginning an article," she explained. She felt self-conscious. She could no longer talk about her troubles with the article without revealing herself to be a disaster. "It's on a farmer, a dairy farmer. Who is supposed to be a genius at cows."

"You must have to go far to find a cow in this part of the country," he said, "unless I am misunderstanding."

He had a very gentle voice. He didn't seem to know much about agriculture. He asked about the size of the farm, the distance from the city, and about the cows—were they gentle? They were very gentle. They were tender with their young. But they weren't really interested in anyone. It made them easier to slaughter: up until the very moment of the act you could imagine they might not notice. Karen twisted open the bottle of water and took a small, polite sip. She was becoming interested in herself again after several weeks of wishing she could be anybody else. Did she like milk very much? Yes, she did, this is how she found the story, she drank the wonderful milk that cost $13 a bottle and then began to investigate where it came from and how it could be so good. It was three o'clock in the afternoon and the grayish winter light looked flat through the plate glass windows. She had a sense of her face as flexible, soft. This was the longest that Karen had talked to a person since Vanessa's birthday party last week where Vanessa had compromised herself with whiskey sodas and made Karen promise never to get back together with Tim, ever, because he was a sneak and a pervert, practically a stalker and she could do so much better, she was better off. Vanessa and Tim had been friends since college, but after the breakup Vanessa said she was choosing Karen. "I'm not saying Tim's a terrible person," she said, "he's a mediocre person. But he's one of those people who won't let up. He thinks he can wear you down, and he can."

When Martin asked her if she'd like to go next door and have a pizza, she didn't think about whether it would be awkward. She thought about how normal it was to talk to someone, to drink coffee, to thrust your face into full view of other faces, to let the daylight grime up your skin. "I think I can take a break," Karen said abstractly, like one being shaken out of deep concentration, "but I'll need to come back afterwards, I have a deadline coming." They put their things into bags and stood up. He tried to carry her bag, but he kept dropping it.

A middle-aged man and woman were sitting at the tables closest to the exit. They sat separately, but had identical laptops. "You know what," Karen heard the man say as she passed by. "I haven't dreamt in a very long time."

In the pizza restaurant, Martin looked five years older. A waiter brought them ice water in green-tinted glasses of pebbled plastic, and straws. Karen watched as Martin tore the tips from the paper casings of the straws and gently pulled them off. He split the remainder of the wrapper down its seam precisely, like he was undressing a doll. She wondered whether this had to do with being German. Karen didn't use the straw he had prepared for her. She lifted the glass to her lips and drank the cold, slightly sour water. Ice tapped against her teeth. She felt like she was going to cry, but then inexplicably she felt okay again. Food was disgusting, but she had to eat it anyway. Martin was telling her that he, too, had been interested in writing for a brief time. He had become involved in film criticism during his time in the media studies program at Humboldt University in Berlin. In those days he used to watch a film each night, walking a mile and a half back home along the Spree River. He liked to see the other regulars there, although he never spoke to them—the old man with the antique briefcase, the young mother who brought her slumbering infant. He thought that he might even write a book on Carl Theodor Dreyer's work, in particular the film *Vampyr*.

"Why Carl Dreyer?" Karen asked.

"Carl Theodor Dreyer," said Martin. "This is like asking 'Why history? What is interesting about history?' It is not a matter of interest. There is no opinion on it."

"I haven't seen *Vampyr*," she said.

"Oh," he replied. "It's quite all right."

In her weeks at Ned Regan's farm, Karen had seen why they called him a genius. With a long, knuckly arm, Ned guided cows from field to shed, weaving them through the gates like huge, slow-moving agility dogs. When yield fell below Ned's expectations, he knew how to adjust the feed, supplementing grass with alfalfa, fenugreek, thistle. With firm pressure on the flank he could signal a cow to slow or stop, with a deep, low groan he could still an anxious mama and she would let him come close and take her knobby calf into his rough hands. In the empty restaurant Martin seemed to be having a nice time. His smile had grown easier, he was marveling at the menu. All of this was locally grown? Here, so close to the city, the marvelous towers of cold, hard glass? He suggested they order the "Bad Girl," a pizza with four different types of cured meat on it, plus smoked cheese and green onions. Over by the register, their waiter was talking to a waitress in a black tank top. "That's terrible," he said, patting the countertop instead of her hand. "That's not all," replied the waitress. Karen told Martin that she would prefer a different pizza. The only meat that she ate these days was beef: somehow, after having spent so much time with the cows, she felt certain that they meant her no harm.

When the pizza came, it was covered in mushrooms. They had the earthy smell of something that has been buried and then dug up. Martin said he would also like a beer, but Karen told him she had to write later. They were the only customers in the whole place, it was too early for dinner. The sky seen through the windows was a pale, even gray as though it had been scrubbed bare. Martin had nice skin. With his small front teeth, he nibbled at a mushroom, seizing it delicately and pulling it from the pizza. He was nice, and he asked good questions. He asked whether Karen had traveled much and if, when she did, she felt like a different person. He asked if she liked to know where her food came from, or whether she preferred to think that it had been created just for her at that moment. He asked if she often met strangers in the coffee shop and then went with them to eat pizza, and she told him honestly that she never had before. She didn't tell him that she hadn't spoken to anyone besides Vanessa in the past week and even that had been strange, stilted and vague as they spoke surrounded by Vanessa's other friends, hard-eyed young women from the world of television news. Martin would be here, in this city, in this neighborhood, for a few more days. He would be completing the project with his friend who also lived in the neighborhood, in a loft building overlooking the motorcycle-themed Biergarten. Perhaps Karen and his friend were neighbors. There was a gallery event on Thursday that she might be interested in attending. Or she could show him some of the other sights of the neighborhood, like the grocery store operated by the

Korean family that also sold martial arts merchandise and kung fu DVDs. Their waiter was no longer talking to the waitress in the black tank top, though they stood near each other still. Martin ordered a large can of beer from the waiter, and when it came Karen ordered one too.

When she went to use the restroom she didn't check her phone. It almost didn't matter to her whether Tim had called, though she had to admit it still mattered. Talking with Vanessa had made her feel that she was nearly ready to forget him completely; all she needed was another week or two. Last time they hung out, only their second time without Tim around, Vanessa had told her about something terrible that he had done to her while they were still in college. In senior year, a large group of their friends had decided to rent a six-bedroom lake house for the weekend. The house had five full-size beds, four cots, and two couches, but the situation was such that different people would still have to bunk together, systematically, to fit everyone into bed at night. This was ideal for Vanessa, who knew that she had a good chance of sharing a bed with Jason, who not only had admitted that he had feelings for her but also really understood why she was interested in broadcast journalism—not because it was the best or most rigorous journalism but because it felt like it was happening in the immediate now. The first night they spooned together in bed, but the next Vanessa drank too much tequila. When she woke up, it wasn't Jason but Tim crawling naked under the covers with her, his pink and sunburned arms reaching up under her nightshirt, rooting around the folds of her flesh, grabbing at her nipples. Even though nothing else happened, Tim told

Jason that they had sex. Jason didn't speak to her again until after graduation. Now Jason was in Hollywood, acting in a popular TV show where he played a high school athlete. Although Vanessa had slept with Tim a few months after that under different circumstances, she had never completely forgiven him for having foreclosed for her the possibility of sleeping with the person she had truly wanted and hoped to sleep with. It was news to Karen that they had slept together. The week after she met Vanessa, she had asked Tim if anything had ever happened between them. He told her nothing had, then he made her apologize to him for asking. It was a fight over this piece of information that had broken them up, and this surprised her: there had been so many fights that left behind no trace or consequence.

When Karen got back to the table, Martin was putting away his phone. "Sorry," said Karen. "It's not a problem," Martin replied. He tried to be warm to her, he reached his hand across the table and placed it near hers. Tim had liked this place, with its stupid pun-filled names for pizzas and its great beer menu. The tank top waitress was humming a different pop song from the one playing over the speakers. Karen and Martin listened to her humming. Neither of them had anything to say.

"You should come for a visit," said Martin.

"Visit?" said Karen.

"In Berlin. It'll be spring soon. There are fantastic clubs," he said.

Karen was surprised. She smiled.

"Maybe I'll visit," she said. She had a vision of herself walking in the sunshine. She was wearing the same clothes, same hairstyle. She felt happy. Was she in Berlin? They drank from their huge cans of beer.

"Are you doing something after this?" Martin asked.

"Well, I need to work," Karen replied.

"Yes, yes," said Martin. "But can you take a break?"

"Well," said Karen, confused, "I might watch a movie."

"Do you want to watch a movie together?" he asked.

"I don't know where," she said. "I just watch movies in my room. I don't even have a TV. It's a small screen."

"It might work," he said.

More people were entering the restaurant now. They had come off work nearby. They were chattering and laughing. They were the loudest thing in the room. Every time someone entered, a frigid draft passed through and made all the customers look around. It was decided that Martin would go to Karen's apartment. Karen felt tired. She wanted to be alone now, but it wasn't fair to want someone around only when you wanted them around. As Martin had grown more relaxed, he had also grown more agitated. When he spoke, he gestured with a pointed finger. They talked about their parents while they waited for the check. Martin's mother was an angel, a kind and very pretty woman who had left him the money to go to graduate school.

"Did she pass away?" Karen asked.

"Away?" asked Martin.

"Passed away," she repeated.

"No," he said sharply. "She is alive." He sounded irritated.

"When we say someone has left money, we usually mean they've passed away," Karen explained.

Martin leaned back in his seat.

"No," he said, more mildly. "Not dead."

Karen thought of her article, of the different scenes she had tried to begin with, none of which were right. She thought of Ned Regan, bending down to grasp a teat infected with mastitis, a persistent and sometimes fatal inflammation of the udder. The teat was black and necrotized and surrounded by other abnormal teats, deeply red and swollen. He pulled at it to show her how the tissue was dead, how the tissue felt nothing. The cow released a tired moan. Because the Regan farm was 100 percent antibiotic-free, cases that weren't identified in time were nearly always fatal. That day Tim had written to her, admitting that he hadn't been honest about his relationship with Vanessa, that he was sorry, that he only failed to mention it because it wasn't important and took place so long ago. Karen felt unhappy. She thought she might cry. Then she felt a little less unhappy. When the waiter brought the check, she noticed that there were small cuts all over his hands, each one scabbed over and neat.

As they left the restaurant, Karen remembered how she had left food out on the kitchen counter hours ago. The sliced deli cheese would still be there, shiny and hard, sweating out beads of grease atop the waxy paper.

Martin and Karen stood in front of her building, a converted warehouse that housed over twenty different lofts on each floor. The lofts were labeled A through V. Though over a hundred people must have lived in her building, Karen had met none of them. When she came upon them in the stairwell she looked away, at the painted gray cement or out the window at the roof of the warehouse across the street. As she looked away they looked at her quizzically, trying to gauge whether she belonged. Martin stood next to Karen as she tried to key in the security code to the front door. She wished that he'd look away while she pushed the buttons in order, but he did not. When the door buzzed and she pulled it open, they stepped into the chilly foyer. He held her hand for a second and then dropped it. The texture and shape of his hand reminded her of a washcloth.

They climbed the steps slowly and without talking much. Through the window you could see a large truck unloading boxes at the doughnut warehouse. Karen stopped at the apartment door. "I may not be much fun," she said, trying to make it sound like a joke and a serious statement at once. "That's all right," said Martin, picking her hand up and holding it longer this time, patting it three times with his free hand. At the end of each workday, after they had finished with dinner and cleaned up the dishes, Ned Regan would sit down at the table with a cool glass of fresh whole milk squeezed from his favorite cow, Lainey. Ned used to say that it was this daily glass of milk that reminded him why he should get up the next morning and do it all over again. He also said that it had cured him of acid reflux and sleep apnea. Ned was a picture of health, his cheeks ruddy and tanned, his teeth straight and the strong hands clutching a column of pure thick white. But as he brought the glass to his mouth and began sucking up the creamy, frothy top with his sun-chapped lips, Karen always fought the desire to look away. She could hear the wet slap of tongue against liquid, the greedy glug of the throat as it tried to swallow as much as it could and then swallow more. When he had finished the entire glass and breathed a sigh of relief, she saw the white ghost of milkfat on his upper lip and couldn't help but think of him as an infant, a gigantic calloused infant.

The apartment opened up onto the disorderly kitchen. The kitchen was as she knew it would be: dishes undone, sliced cheese splayed out in the open. There was a bowl of cereal sitting out on top of the stove that she had forgotten to eat. Martin was looking at the spices on the rack and nodding at them. He pointed at one.

"Very nice," he said.

"What?" asked Karen.

"Turmeric," he answered.

Karen crumpled the pile of paper and cheese into a ball and stuffed it in the trash.

"Would you give me a tour?" asked Martin. From where he stood he could already see almost the entirety of the apartment, which was arranged in a straight line from the door toward a large back window. The only thing he couldn't see into was the bedroom, a small closed-in room with walls all around. It had a small window onto the rest of the apartment. "Like a cave," the realtor had said.

"Sure," said Karen, washing her hands. She dried them on a paper towel.

She showed him the kitchen table and the bathroom with its goldfish-printed shower curtain. She showed him the couch and the heating duct and the bookshelf with its array of old schoolbooks and novels. She showed him a plant that she had been given by a friend when she moved into this apartment. She stood outside the bedroom and explained how it was very difficult for light to find its way inside, which made it a good place to sleep and write. Her desk was inside the small lightless room, and sitting at it occasionally made Karen feel so desperate that she went over to the bed and fell asleep instead.

"What do you think you'd like to watch?" Karen asked.

"What?" asked Martin.

"What kind of movie do you want to see. I have some of everything," she said.

"Oh," said Martin, "I'll watch what you want."

"I don't have any Dreyer," she said.

"Do you usually watch in bed?" he asked, pointing up at the lofted mattress.

"Sometimes I watch at the desk," she said, pointing at the desk.

"Okay," he said, "the desk."

"There's another chair in the kitchen," Karen said. She went to get it, but Martin stopped her.

"Should I take off my shoes?" he asked.

"Oh," she said. "Yes."

He bent over and untied each shoe before pulling it off. His shoes were leather sneakers with a letter B on the side. As she watched him, Karen could see that his hands were shaking badly. He had trouble holding the little ends of the shoelaces as he tugged to undo them. He straightened his body up.

"I think one chair is fine," said Martin, sitting down in the rolling desk chair. It squeaked. They looked at each other.

"I'd like to sit, too," Karen said, her arms stiff.

Martin leaned forward and took her hands in his, pulling her toward him. His hands were shaking so much that her hands shook too. Their hands jittered together like they were on a bumpy car ride through the countryside.

"One is fine," said Martin again, as he pulled her down onto his lap.

Tim used to say that Karen was the smartest person he had ever met. This meant something to Karen because in her own family, she had never even been close to the smartest person. She was always the weak thinker, the vague thinker, and these days thoughts came to her damaged in transit, one piece now and one piece several hours later, its counterpart already forgotten. Tim used to tell stories about how dumb Vanessa was. Vanessa was a successful associate news producer and therefore not literally dumb, but she had done some things in college. Once she was tricked into skinny-dipping and nobody else went in the water. Once she paid $1,200 to buy a star that would be named after herself, and it was a scam. She used to think that global warming was due to the rise of air conditioners, pumping hot air out into the climate in exchange for cold, and would correct itself as people grew more used to the hotter temperatures and used their air-conditioning units less. None of it mattered much to Karen. She had only known Vanessa for six months, though she had been with Tim for almost two years. She liked Vanessa because Vanessa liked her. Vanessa liked her because they both read the big thick Sunday newspaper all through the following week, and felt roughly the same way about the quality of each article. At the end of the night Vanessa was often slung over her shoulders, breathing heavily near her ear and telling Tim that he was so lucky, so lucky and he should stop being such an asshole.

Karen felt the sharp blades of Martin's thighbones digging into the backs of her thighs. She squirmed on his lap, but that made it hurt more. He was like a man made of metal, inhospitable. Beneath her she felt something moving, twitching, a curious subterranean animal trying to find its way into the light.

Karen pushed herself up from the chair and walked to the far end of the room, but it was not a large room. She turned and looked at Martin, who looked confused.

"I just wanted to watch a movie," said Karen. She was holding her elbows in her hands and her arms were crossed.

"I," said Martin. "I've enjoyed talking to you very much."

"Yes," she said. "That's fine."

They were six feet apart.

"Would you like me to leave?" Martin asked.

Karen nodded. "Yes," she said.

Karen didn't want to stand there and watch while Martin put his shoes back on, but it was a small room and he was blocking the door. With one hand he formed a loop with the end of the shoelace. With the other he drew the other lace around and under. His hands were still shaking. He pulled the laces tight and stepped out into the apartment. The afternoon light was still cold and bright, but it was getting dimmer. She stood there and watched while he collected his bag, his jacket. Sometimes she looked away but there was nothing to look at. After he put on his jacket and gloves, she grabbed his forearm and squeezed it with her hand. Then she tried to slide her cheek next to his, but she forgot to make the kissing sound. She grabbed his forearm again and let it go. She had forgotten how to be a person.

At the door Martin turned around.

"I have your phone number," he said.

She nodded.

"I'll call you to come out on Thursday," he said.

"Okay," said Karen, and she closed the door behind him.

In the empty apartment, Karen sat on the chair by the kitchen table and shook silently. Her mother had a saying. Whenever you had given your all, she would tell you that it was time to "let the legumes grow." This meant recognizing that you had nothing left to do because you had nothing left. You were a fallow field from which nothing more was going to come. Your task was to lay back and wait for the spring, when something might once again grow from you. Karen tried to sway back and forth, but it was not a sturdy chair. She sat still and closed her eyes. She had been doing okay at Ned Regan's farm until she saw how they separated the cows from their calves. A milk cow only lactates if she has recently given birth, and this means that each dairy cow must be bred back roughly once a year. Calving is continual, and crucial. At the same time, the calf must be displaced so that it does not consume the bulk of the milk that is to be collected and sold. Ned Regan's policy was to allow the cow and calf a week together, plenty of time to absorb the colostrum, an antibody-rich milk that mother cows produce in the first few days after birth. Most farmers only allowed three days, and industrial farms took the babies within hours. In the first few days after birth, Ned allowed the mothers to lick their babies dry. He lifted the spindly calves up to their mothers' teats if they were too weak to find them themselves, he guided the teats into their wet mouths. But on the seventh day, Karen watched as Ned and his dairy hands set up a series of pens bounded by elec-trified wire. As the lot was herded through the pasture, the calves passed under a low-lying wire while their mothers re-mained on the other side. Once most of the calves had passed through, Ned and his helpers strung two more wires to close off the breach. The few calves that remained unsorted were sorted out by hand. They hauled them up into the back of a pickup and drove them away. The mothers cried out for their calves all through the night, and the night after, and the night after that. "Why don't the mothers fight when you take them away?" Karen asked Ned once he returned from dropping the calves off in town. "They feel safe in groups," Ned answered. "That's why they don't spook when you walk them to the slaughterhouse."

Karen saw a text message on her phone. It was from Martin. She could see the shadow he cast in the thin slit of light coming from under the front door. He was still there, pacing back and forth. She never wanted to see him again. Martin had experienced only one truly uncivil encounter in the history of his romantic life. In college, a girl he had been sleeping with and whom he liked very much had stopped calling him and then stopped talking to him in the halls. When he saw her in the university buildings, she walked by him not as though he were a stranger, but as though he were not there at all. Later a friend told him she had spread the rumor that he cheated on her with someone from his economics class. This was not only false, but mystifyingly so. Martin knew nobody in his economics class. He couldn't even name one female who took the class with him. The situation was bizarre, the girl's behavior inexplicable. This experience impressed upon Martin the view that most women were unknowable. As he said: "Women will sometimes burn a thing just to watch it burn." Although he was occasionally lonely, he tried not to be bitter. He thought there were good things in the world that he would encounter by chance. He was only thirty-five, and he believed it would happen whether or not he changed himself significantly.

Karen went back to her room and closed the door. There was very little light now coming in through the bedroom window. She climbed the ladder up to her bed and wrapped herself in the duvet. She slept in a lofted bed, like a child. She was always afraid that she would roll off it in the middle of the night and break her neck on her own bureau dresser. This fear woke her sometimes, and she'd stretch out her arm to feel for the end of the bed before rolling her body inward to where the mattress met the wall. A psychology graduate student that Karen had met at a party listened to her description of the milk calf weaning and became excited. "Don't you think it's so interesting," said the graduate student from Austria, "that you say the cows 'cried'? We project so much onto animals. You hear the sounds as crying, as if they were human beings with our emotions, when it was probably something different, more like a call." Karen thought about Vanessa at her party the other night. She was loudly drunk, the Vanessa of college stories instead of the one who spoke tautly about the people she competed with at work and got annoyed when it took too long for the check to come. "I just want to say that I'm sorry," she said, placing her hand on Karen's back and then removing it. "For a long time I never knew you were dating Tim, or actually I never knew he was dating you. You know I like you. So I just never knew. You only became real once I saw you. And then after I met you I just wanted you to like me back, so I didn't want to say anything. It wasn't about you, I promise, or even Tim. It's just easy to keep doing a thing once you've already done it before." Karen, already drunk on only two gin and tonics, was confused but understood that they were both engaged in an emotional interaction. "No," she said, "it's okay. It's weird becoming friends through a guy, I really understand. You've always been great to me."

When Karen finally realized what it was that Vanessa had been trying to tell her, she rolled onto her side and pretended she was asleep. It was difficult to feel as though any of this had really happened. It was as though she had opened up a magazine and were reading about it all. She felt sympathy for those involved, but ultimately these were people that she would never meet in real life. When she began feeling again, mostly she felt dumb. She was definitely not the smartest person in any group of people. She was a creature. That night on Ned Regan's farm, she had lain awake listening to the sounds of the mother cattle out calling in the fields. They moaned for their young, for the beasts that they had pushed out of their bodies, hooves and hard parts and all. Their voices were low, round, masculine. They sounded like trains, urgent trains, calling out for a place that they would not reach. Deep into the night she heard a knock on her door. Ned Regan eased it open. Some light from a far-off room leaked into her guest bedroom with the small cot and the nightstand. He stood there looking at her in bed.

"Hello?" Karen said, asking.

"I'm just checking to see," said Ned Regan.

"Is everything okay?" Karen asked.

"Everything's okay," said Ned. "I just wanted to see if you needed something."

There was silence.

"Are you sure there's nothing you need?" Ned asked again.

"No, really, no," she said, and she tried to sound like it was all settled. After Ned closed the door and she heard his footsteps moving farther and farther away, she looked out the window. It was a brilliant moon with a painfully white halo. The surface of the moon was disfigured with a gray shape that looked like a broken flower.

Karen lay on her side in her own bed with her eyes closed, facing the wall. She thought about Tim's body and Vanessa's body locked together while she existed someplace else, knowing and feeling things about Tim. She thought about the first year dating Tim, when he had been sleeping with Vanessa and at the same time telling Karen about the intercourse map they had drawn of her freshman year. She wanted to call him ten times in a row and yell at him, but her phone was in the other room. She felt sad, but she hadn't cried all day. She thought that crying would actually be a good thing right now. It seemed normal to react. Whoever Martin had been, he had probably been a normal person. He was probably having the normal reaction right now, and she had caused it. She felt bad for confusing him. She thought it might be fair to cry for him. But it wasn't until she thought of the mother cows in the pasture the day after the weaning, wandering around singly in the naked sunshine, still trying to call out in their hoarse, broken voices for the young ones that were still missing, that she was finally able to make herself cry—a little bit for all of the calves, but mostly for herself.

Choking Victim

When she was younger she could be alone for weeks and never realize that it was time to miss another person, time to call another person on the phone. Now she found herself missing anybody she could think of. Nobody had warned her that watching her husband hold her baby with such care, their faces opened wordlessly onto one another in admiration, would make her feel so clumsy. She climbed the staircase up to the bed and lay on her side, her gut and womb positioned directly above the space where the two of them took their alone time together. They might be in love with one another, but her body was the causal link. Mentally she was older than ever, tired in the morning as though it were already the end of the day, but this longing for others was a smooth pink patch where she felt as raw as a child.

Her name was Karen and she was thirty-two years old, but she had a much younger face. She had hair to her shoulders and a body like a girl's, with knobby joints. When she pushed her baby through the park in a bulky red stroller, people watched her with curiosity and pity. In her plain but adult clothes she looked like a teenage nanny, someone from another country who was underpaid and exploited. She was always being mistaken for a foreigner.

. . .

For the next two weeks her husband would be in China, watching over the construction of a large new building, a government library built directly above a portion of the local river. Once the building was complete, the most beautiful and formerly accessible part of the river would be hidden away from the view of ordinary citizens. She felt lonelier without him around, but while he was away she could have her own time alone with her daughter. In the hot patch of sunlight on the sofa she drew the soft baby toward her. She rested the small, heavy body on her lap and turned it so that the head lay in the cup of her hand. She examined its face, an abbreviation of her own. Where the eye area and mouth area met was a strange new nose unlike any she had seen in her own family or her husband's. They had named the baby Lila, a name that was impossible for an infant to occupy, hoping that she would grow into it.

Dressed in lavender stripes, the baby looked up at her calmly and shut her mouth. By six months, infants were supposed to babble freely—but hers had said almost nothing. A traumatic or hostile home environment could obstruct an infant's development, but Karen was confident that she and her husband weren't guilty of that. They got along well, and when they fought it was in the style that he preferred—sentences clipped, reasonable but with a harsh and colorless tone. There was nothing there that could harm a baby, Karen told herself, especially one that didn't even understand words. Karen and her husband had met when they were young and working in a bigger city. One of the best things about him had been his face, which was handsome but not overly so. It was a healthy, normal face, and when you looked at it you could imagine the person it belonged to doing any number of harmless things—pedaling on a stationary bicycle, assembling a sandwich, listening to music while driving a car. Just looking at that face was enough to make Karen feel that she had peered into every crevice of his personality. But when he was away for too long, she found it difficult to remember how the different parts of his face fit together, even though they had been married for almost five years now.

Outside the window, men walked past berating faceless, bodiless voices on their phones. Cars rolled by so slowly that she could hear the engine whine in the deep center of the machine. It was time to begin speaking to your baby, the parenting books warned. At all moments of the day she should be describing the world and linking objects with the words that identified them. Without a steady stream of well-articulated adult speech an infant might lag in its development, not only in language use but also in its understanding of objects, concepts, and reasoning. Her daughter would essentially remain an animal. Karen wanted to begin speaking a steady stream of well-articulated language to her baby, but it was difficult to articulate. Sometimes when she sat still and listened to the inside of her mind she became distracted by the sound of a gentle rushing, like water from a faucet.

From the neighboring apartment came a noisy coughing, muffled by the wall between. The cougher was an unlikable retiree who the neighbors referred to by his last name, Puldron. Each day she watched through the sighthole in her door as he shuffled over to her stack of mail on the entryway table to paw piece by piece through her bills and catalogs, his blunt fingers pinching and creasing the flimsy photos of stylish outdoor furniture. Sometimes she heard the sound of a page being ripped out and folded over and over into a tight packet, and when she cross-referenced her mutilated catalog with the one on view online, she saw that hers was now missing an image of a picnic basket or an industrial-style upholstered coffee table with wheels. Was Puldron trying to keep her from buying those objects and putting them in her home to make her family complete?

The coughing continued, louder and more urgent. It grew and solidified simultaneously, like a skyscraper seen from an approaching car. Again and again Puldron emptied his throat of sound, and Karen could hear the wet clutch of the throat tube. A muscular *gk* shuddered at the edge of the sound, the snag of choking. He hacked at the thing trapped in him until she found herself standing up, still holding her baby, her body moving to do something it hadn't decided on yet: she had never spoken to Puldron, had never wanted to, maybe he'd take it as some sort of aggression. She looked down at the small ears of her daughter, unavoidably open to the world, eagerly capturing the sounds of the choking man and turning them inward to shape her soft, growing mind.

Karen waited. The coughing turned to a wheeze, culminated in silence.

She went over to the wall and pushed her ear to it. Nothing stirred behind the white wall, no spasm of mouth or throat. It had only been a minute or two, or maybe a couple more, since the choking had started. She bumped her elbow weakly against the wall, arms full of daughter. "Are you choking?" she shouted.

If it was true that the smallest unit of stimuli could have a formative effect, then listening to the death of her neighbor only a few feet away in his apartment was bound to do horrible things to future Lila. There could be pyromania, cutting of the skin, morbid fascination with death. Teenage perils that Karen could hardly believe she had experienced herself, in her own past—thinking about it was like hearing a funny story about something you had done while you were drunk, an event you had to trust had been real but which now no longer lived even in your own mind. The worst part was, she had already let it happen: Lila had heard the whole grisly sound track. Karen needed to show her something beautiful immediately—a swan, a fountain. She propped the baby on the sofa and went around the apartment grabbing things and throwing them in an oversize, floppy bag. She put the bag on the stroller, buckled the little body into the seat, breathing in spurts. At the door she realized that she should have called an ambulance. She took the phone from her pocket. It was too late, wasn't it?

Karen pulled the door open to escape and found Puldron, alive, standing by the mail table. Her reaction was relief, then irritation. The damage to Lila's psyche had already been done.

Puldron exhaled wetly and continued his work as she pushed by him. He didn't move; there was plenty of room for the frantic woman to get by with her ugly stroller. He flipped the page, flipped the page again, until he found something workable. With small fine movements he tugged at the paper, tearing along the crease buried in the booklet's stapled spine. It was a picture of a complicated bowl, asymmetrical and made of iron: an object with gravity. The bowl had a vaguely birdlike shape, like it could glide from on high. At the same time, it was large and surely very heavy. In the trough of the bowl, some idiot had placed a couple of puny lemons, shattering the remarkable somberness of the piece. The salespeople behind these photos wanted to make you believe you could live a happy homemaker's life with these objects, but in fact the best thing an object could do was to remove you from your life, offer you a portal into the world of pure form. When handling a truly well-balanced piece, you could feel its proportions in your body, in the rightness of your hands traveling its surface. But it was no use speaking of pure form with the people you came across. This was an age in which everything in the world emerged from the womb with a price already stamped upon it.

While there was nothing exactly wrong with the park, there was not much right with it either. The light-colored grass was brittle to the touch and though it looked like it needed water, between bristly tufts the earth was soft and muddy. To her right and left loose bands of teenage boys and girls shoved one another, the girls letting out terrifying screams and then laughing at Karen when she turned to look at them. "That lady's never seen someone have fun in her entire life," one girl said to another. "She's like, I'm scared!" the other girl replied. As she shoved the ugly red stroller over the chalky path Karen wondered what type of body language she was projecting to the surrounding world. When she had left the hospital with Lila in her arms it seemed as though she had stepped onto a different planet.

People looked at her now only to get out of her way. If someone stopped to speak to her, linger on her, it was always a
woman—a woman with advice on how to mother, a woman
who wanted to know the baby's name or age. She had
emerged into a world made only of women, and although
they used a friendly tone they spoke to her like a new em-
ployee whose incompetence was guaranteed.

Karen was surprised to see herself push past the fountain she had intended to show Lila. But what would they do
with the fountain anyhow? Crouch alongside it, peer over its
gray lip into the fake blue water at a smattering of pennies,
twigs, the drifting body-casings of insects. Lift the baby up
and dangle her over the surface so that she could swipe at
the dirty water with her hand. In the larger sense, all of this
would be forgotten by the child almost as it was happening. Even now, as something inside her mother unspooled
nearby, Lila seemed unchanged. She didn't cry, she let out
only a prolonged gurgle as her body shook, propelled over
gravel. Her blue eyes reached eagerly for the green grass,
the rough stones. Karen took Lila's silence as license to continue: the walk was loosening her, it erased the ugliness of
Puldron's mouth, the compacted feeling that came with
being at home.

Instead of the fountain, she would take her baby to see the
water. But there was no real water in this city, Karen thought
to herself, water you could sink your body into to feel more
alive. They left the park and passed the library, the grocery,
an Italian restaurant that Karen hadn't eaten at since she
was in college, visiting a friend. They passed a bodega where
a woman sat on a squat stool, arranging many attractive,

brightly colored oranges so that they covered the misshapen yellowing ones beneath. The other mothers were envious of Lila's personality: she scored very well on the rubrics for head-turning, object memory, and facial recognition, which indicated that she was in the process of developing a high IQ—but she rarely cried or complained, which allowed the other mothers to experience her as a being of pure adorability, a sponge for affection that asked nothing in return. But the daughter that Karen had wanted was a daughter who talked, who chattered, who would help her become more of a human being and who would remake the world for her in her own eyes, a daughter she hoped she would have in the future. "I love you just like you are," she said out loud.

In Karen's grip the stroller's handlebar was shaking, twisting left and right and left, as though there were someone holding on to the front of the stroller, pulling it. Lila's soft white face began to crumple, from its open center came a high wail as the contraption shook her body. Karen stopped and went to see what had gone wrong. As the apparatus tipped forward it drew a lazy arc in the air, moving slow and quick at the same time, making it look like the baby was diving forward. By falling onto her knees and thrusting her arms blindly out, Karen was just able to keep Lila from hitting the sidewalk.

Karen looked at the stroller, at the child. The inside of her head felt slow with panic, and the sound of her daughter crying muffled her thoughts. The wheel had come off, she could see it a few yards back, and who knew where the piece that held it on had been lost? The stroller would have to be left behind; she couldn't carry it and the baby both. At the same time, the stroller was so expensive she knew she would have to come back for it. It had been a high-quality model, brightly colored and flashy. It had a chassis of feather-light, heat-resistant titanium, and its parts had been manufactured in Germany by a company that made some of the less important parts of airplanes. She and her husband had agreed it was the best model, safe and firmly made. When she wheeled it around, with its geometric-patterned diaper bag and its plastic frame shiny as a fast food playground, she felt bumbling, cartoonish, gaudy like a clown.

Karen gathered Lila, red with tears, into her arms and began walking. It was only a few moments later that she remembered to think of a place to go.

In the café in the neighborhood where people came mostly to shop, there were only two other customers: a young man on a laptop, his large head squeezed between headphones, and an older woman eating a salad, who might have been a young grandmother. She sat down at the table farthest from both of them. Her arms ached, and she had blisters where heel and instep met the straps of her sandals. She felt guilty. She didn't want to go back for the stroller, but to buy a new one would symbolize to her husband that she was unable to keep valuable objects in her possession. "Karen," he'd said tenderly when she lost a good sweater that she'd just bought, "You're a net with one big hole in it. Everything just slips through you." When she got up from the sofa and prepared to leave the house with the new stroller, certain to be similarly ugly and large, she knew she'd feel his eyes on her, showing and stifling concern at the same time.

With her gaze fixed on an empty corner, Karen adopted the flat facial expression of someone reading, though she had nothing to look at. She slid off her shoes. She just wanted to drink the sweet, tepid tea and think of nothing. But from the corner of her eye, she saw the older woman watching her between brief, performative glances at a magazine that had recently been rolled up into a small, tight tube. As it lay on the table, it curled slowly in on itself once again. Karen looked over at her, and looked away again too late.

"Did you borrow that shirt from someone?" the older woman asked, smiling toothily and leaning toward Karen.

"No," Karen said. It was her own shirt. Karen turned to Lila and pretended that she was doing something involving and important with her. Taking a corner of Lila's soft yellow blanket, she dabbed the little face gently, over and over again.

"Well, it's very nice," said the voice from behind her back.

Karen felt a tug on her sleeve and turned her head. The woman next to her was rubbing the fabric between her long finger and her thumb. The shirt was too big. It was a cotton blend, covered in a garish print of lilies and strawberries. In fact, Karen hated this shirt.

"Thank you," she said stiffly, holding still.

"Has she started to say her words yet?" the woman asked, indicating Lila with a point of her fork. She leaned back and stabbed at her salad, making space for Karen to sit up straight in the seat.

"It's too early," Karen admitted, "too early for babbling, even."

"That's a lonely time. I know it. You two are together all

day long, and there's nobody even to say 'mm-hmm.'" The woman laughed.

Karen nodded slowly.

"I'm Linda. How old are you, honey?" said Linda, holding out her hand.

"Thirty-two," Karen answered, wiping her sweaty palm on her shorts and squeezing Linda's outstretched hand for an instant. Linda smiled and nodded as though she wasn't surprised. In her green silk blouse and pink patterned scarf, she was either somebody who understood colors very well or someone who didn't understand them at all.

"And you feel a million years old inside, am I right?" Linda smiled winningly, her teeth sharply white in the dim lighting. Linda reminded Karen of a TV mother, someone who always had good advice and probably had never been bored, anxious, or confused in her life.

"I don't know," Karen said. "I feel *strange*."

"Well, don't we all." Linda shrugged as, wrapped in blankets at her side, a long, escalating cry began to break from the baby. "You live life one way for, what, thirty years, you've just finally, barely gotten used to the way life is, and then BAM!" Linda swiped her finger against wailing Lila's mouth. Lila quieted instantly. "They tell you that you gotta start learning life all over again. BAM! Isn't that right?" Linda winked at Karen, and wiped the front and back of her hand on a napkin.

"How did you *do* that?" Karen exclaimed, truly impressed.

"Oh, just an old family trick. Old, old trick," Linda said, leaning in. "A teensy dab of butter on the lips. Tamps them down like lambs." Linda was different from other mothers Karen had met: when she gave advice, it wasn't stuffy. She was full of stories. For every frustration Karen named, Linda knew someone who in fact had gone through just that problem herself. Linda was a sort of freelance psychoanalyst, consultant, therapist, whatever you please. Diverse but well-respected people, she said, had sought her services for issues ranging from their child's learning disability to what type of second career they should take on. She had just got these great new business cards printed on 100 percent cotton paper, the real thing, only she didn't have any with her today.

As for Karen, what she was dealing with right now was completely natural. Linda pounded her fist on the table in a fun way, to make the point: "It's easy to lose yourself in a kid, even easier if you love them. Your husband comes back, he's tired, you're tired, in the end all you have time for is a little kiss on the mouth and a conversation about what the little baby ate that day. Nobody sees you as *yourself* anymore, only as the walking mouthpiece for that cute bud of flesh. But let me tell you, it gets easier. I know it." Karen tried to think of what her identity-restoring ritual might be. Her feet ached, her shoes were sweaty. At her side, Lila reached out a small hand for the soiled napkin on the table, grasped it vaguely, let it slip back.

"But you can't let yourself get down about not feeling one hundred percent of the time like the new person you're supposed to be," Linda added with a concerned tone to her voice, her bangs bobbing up and down as she spoke. "It's those expectations, honey. They'll drive you insane."

Karen nodded. Then she remembered the stroller. She had been sitting in the café for more than an hour. Linda's salad was long gone.

"Oh god," Karen said. "I have to go back."

"Go back where?" Linda asked, distracted.

"For the stroller. Part of it broke, the wheel's off, I can't put the baby back in it. Someone's going to take it if I leave it there too long." Karen didn't trust the people of this city, the city in which she lived. In her last city, she had smiled or waved when she saw strangers looking at her.

"Oh, don't worry about it! I'll watch the baby," Linda said, waving her hands in the air to show it was no big deal.

Karen hesitated.

"Look, honey," Linda said, "you haven't got a choice. Life's like that sometimes—you gotta take care of business. You're going to go do your business and come right back, and I'll be right here with the little one, reading my magazine. It's the only way."

"You're sure?" Karen asked.

"Yes, yes, yes," said Linda warmly. "Just go, I'll tend to her every need."

"I'll just be fifteen minutes," said Karen, embarrassed.

"Yes, yes, yes," said Linda. "Get out of here."

Karen picked up her tote and looked down at Lila, still reaching for the napkin, still failing. Karen took the napkin and folded it into a small square, which she slipped into the bag. "I'll be gone for a moment," she said to the infant in an upbeat, gentle voice, "and then I'll be back." She thought. "It means nothing," she added, tenderly. As she stepped out the door, she looked back. She expected to see Linda smiling toothily, holding Lila's little hand and waving it around in a semblance of good-bye. Instead, Linda was rooting around in her handbag for something. Linda and Lila: those names sounded better together than Karen and Lila. What would it signify if Lila chose to unfurl her first words in front of a kind stranger, rather than her own mother?

Outdoors the sun made her squint, and the air smelled of cars. In a similar situation, her husband would have found a way to reclaim the stroller without losing sight of the baby. He had always been good with logistics, one of those people who behave as though they have the instruction manual for the world. Since they had the baby, this quality in him had been exaggerated. Her husband seemed crisper and clearer as he took on his new role: his jaw was better defined, and when he moved around the kitchen, putting towel and coffee mugs back in their places, his gestures had mimelike precision. She was amazed to see him come into focus. These were days full of details to be cataloged, remembered. But sometimes she had the feeling that she had come into focus for her husband too, and what he saw puzzled him.

The night they brought Lila home, Karen had folded a soft striped blanket in half and then in half again, making a soft bed for Lila so she could sleep between their bodies at night. As she placed it on the mattress and pressed into it a baby-shaped depression, her husband walked in. He lunged toward the bed and grabbed the blanket from her as if it were a burning thing. "What do you think you're doing?" he asked, his voice rough. "Babies die that way," he said, and hurled the blanket at the wall to make his point. After they had turned out the lights, he rolled over and covered her in a slew of silent kisses before falling asleep. That night Lila woke from a dream that had made her cry. She wished that she had given birth to something that was impossible to injure, a stone or a stomachful of water. In the dark of the room, the striped blanket lay balled on the floor, its rounded shape full of inner folds and shadows.

As Karen walked back toward the corner where she had abandoned the stroller, she realized that, for all Linda's talk on mothering and its pressures, she had never said explicitly that she had children of her own. For all Karen knew, Linda was as bad at it as she was.

The stroller was intact, its wheel still lying in a patch of marigolds several feet back. Nothing was missing from it except for a few energy bars and a handkerchief from the side pouch, which showed that somebody willing to steal had decided that the bulky vehicle was not worth the trouble. The blisters on Karen's feet had spread to the thick skin of the sole, and she knew she wouldn't make it back to the café unless she wrapped her foot up. Even so, she felt oddly good as she dragged the stroller behind her: a stranger watching from across the street might have described her as "full of purpose." She felt as if Linda had said something that she herself had wished to say for some time. She had to find herself, inside herself, if she was ever going to feel connected again to the things she did all day. She thought about a friend she once had, who she no longer knew, and the long e-mails they used to write each other during their freshman year, describing at weekly intervals precisely how they felt college was changing them, as though logging this data meticulously could keep it all within their control. "I'm leaving you this trail of crumbs so you can find me and return me to myself if I wander too far away." She couldn't remember which one of them had written that junk line. Now her friend was living in Hollywood, a recovering heroin addict who never returned anybody's calls. Last year she had stolen a mutual acquaintance's car and tried to drive it out across state lines into Nevada to do who knows what. From the police station in the desert town she had used her one phone call to leave a message on Karen's voice mail. It said: *Hi, honey. Something wonderful's happened. I finally figured out who I'm supposed to be. I'm beautiful and wise, when I say something it opens people's hearts. The bad news is, I messed up, now I'm the wrong person. But still, I wish you could see me now! Peace and light!* Karen hadn't heard from her since.

She left the stroller outside, leaning on its empty titanium hub outside a drugstore, and limped inside. At the sound of the doors sliding open, the cashier at the counter looked up at her, then dismissed her immediately. The cashier was carving little marks into the checkout counter with a small, pointy pair of scissors in her hand. Karen limped past lightbulbs and window cleaner, full of possibility. Even here, in these boring and overlit aisles, her new good mood made it feel as though anything could happen: she could run into a friend or an ex-lover, she could receive an important phone call, she could have an important thought that would make her whole situation apparent to herself. She stood in front of the bandages and Band-Aids, taking in all their myriad shapes and colors—clear, nude, cloth-covered, breathably plastic, patterned with race cars and cartoon dolphins. She read the backs of the boxes: all the energy and force she would next use to find herself she directed toward this first decision, a practice decision. To her right, a man watched her, his hands in his pockets. He had a nice face with big teeth and ears. When you looked at his face, you could see right through it to the one he had as a little boy. It was easy to imagine him hanging upside down on a swing or standing in front of a rosebush, swatting at it with a broken-off stick. Karen saw him staring at her. She thrust forward a package of Band-Aids.

"Are you looking for these?" she demanded.

"Ah, no, sorry," he said. He paused. "It's just, I think I know you." He had a look on his face like he was waiting for her to complete a sentence.

"From where?" Karen asked. She looked more closely at his whole person. He wore a white button-down shirt. She had always had trouble recognizing people she knew when they dressed up for work.

He named the college in Connecticut that she had gone to. He had been a film major—the film program had changed since he'd gone there, he told her, it used to deal in concrete skills, the mechanics of shooting and editing a film. Now it was mostly a place for people who liked movies to argue over the degree to which a given movie should be liked. Sometimes they invited him back to give a talk and he thought about refusing but in the end he did it anyway because if he could, in his brief thirty-minute talk, impart any advice on how one manipulates the substance of film, he felt that it was his duty. Karen nodded. She relaxed. With his patronizing tone and his floppy brown hair, he was just the sort of person she used to listen to at parties, trying to think of intelligent, psychologically driven questions to ask while she took small sips from a cup of lukewarm beer. She had always been interested in this type of person: in their arrogance, they reminded her of the stylized, opinionated person she might have become if she had been a man.

"How about you?" he asked abruptly, as if she had vanished suddenly and just now reappeared.

"Well," Karen said, "I'm still writing."

"That's great. What do you write?" He had an interested but slightly lost expression on his face.

Like before, she wrote essays. She had written profiles of well-known people—actresses and an artist who sculpted glaciers out of man-made and toxic materials. She had written a long reported article on water sanitation. She had ghostwritten a book by a comedian whose awkward jokes about foreigners were obsolete; all that was left to him was to cash in on the stories he still had of performing with people whose more robust fame persisted to this day.

As Karen spoke, she saw that her old classmate was impressed by the things she had accomplished. She felt content. Talking about work had always made her feel more like herself. He asked thoughtful questions, and she answered them, taking up almost all the space in the conversation. Something in her was eager to expand, to monopolize, to be casually selfish in the way that others often were with her. She felt free, in an old, almost-forgotten way. The happiest week of her life had been in college, the summer after junior year. She had stayed in town working at the library, where she cataloged old, miscellaneous photos according to the objects or themes they contained: Fanaticism, Rhinoceros, Etiquette. At the end of August, students who had also spent the summer in town went home to visit their families for a week or two, but Karen's family was on vacation. So she worked unsupervised in the frosty archive, and after work she jogged five miles to an old railway bridge over the river where she dangled her feet and looked down, watching trash and swaths of plant debris pass below her, borne by the current. When her mother called, she turned her phone facedown and left it there. She would call back several hours later, once she was sure her family was all asleep.

She talked and he nodded. Talking was easy, as it used to be when she was younger and as it would be again and again in the future. This town, which was foreign, would become home, and home would slip again into foreignness. It was only in this small sliver of her life that she would be lonely, and it would pass. But then Karen noticed that he was looking at her more intently than before. She looked away, a reflex.

"Listen," he said seriously. "I'm glad you're not still upset, but I wanted to apologize."

"Apologize for what?" Karen asked.

"You know, for what happened that last year of school." He picked a box of toothpaste up from the shelf, glanced at it, and put it back down.

Karen searched her college memories earnestly for times

when she had been wronged. Most of her life, she felt, had been spent alone in rooms.

"I don't know," she said.

"For the video. I hear it messed you up." Karen could tell he was annoyed that she was making him reassemble the whole situation in front of her in words. "The video of you," he said, "the one I used for class. I know it seemed exploitative, but the idea was to implicate myself. About being male in the cultural moment of the sex tape."

"No," Karen said. "I don't think anything like that's happened to me."

He looked at her in disbelief.

"I don't think I'm who you're thinking of," Karen said slowly. "When exactly were you there?"

It became clear that he had graduated several years after her: they hadn't even overlapped. She had a young face for her age, or he had an old one. They stood in the toothpaste-and-Band-Aid aisle feeling uncomfortable. To Karen he was worse than a stranger: she knew with certainty that something weird lurked inside him. He sensed her change in attitude and stuck his hands back in his pockets. "What did you mean, 'the cultural moment of the sex tape'?" Karen asked. "What did you think would happen if you apologized?" He didn't seem to hear her. Already he seemed a mile away—he was closing up as she watched.

"What did you do?" Karen asked. She stared at him.

"I don't remember," he said unconvincingly. "It was forever ago."

Karen suddenly realized that she hadn't thought of her

husband at all in more than an hour. Had he thought of her, even once?

The sun was setting behind the crosshatching of oak trees as Karen pushed the empty, tilting stroller toward the café as quickly as she could. The sight of the intent, ferocious-looking woman with the empty stroller alarmed the people she passed, but Karen didn't notice. She was truly ready to go home. It seemed incredible to her that just a few hours earlier she had thought that staying in that apartment for another second could kill her. Now she knew that she would become irreparably warped if she spent another minute out here. She felt as if she were deep underwater, desperately stroking up toward the surface, toward light and air. She had no idea how far away it might be.

She'd get back to the café, thank Linda for her time, and hurry her baby home. Home was still a safe space. Everything had gone well there in the end. Puldron was alive, he hadn't choked at all, not completely. And even if he had, the choking was just another corporeal encounter, the body articulating itself around the obstacle of that which choked it. It didn't mean anything more than that. The word *express*, derived from the medieval Latin *expressare*, meant to "press out" or "obtain by squeezing." The word had once been used figuratively as a term for extortion. It was possible that to cough, to choke, was the root of all speech: the urgent need to evacuate something whose internality threatened to kill you. To express yourself or be expressed by extruding words. It was just a bodily function, like sweating or throwing up. Sometimes you felt relief afterward, but there was no point in doing it unless you had to. In light of this, Lila would speak on her own time, when the small, mild experiences she was accumulating finally coalesced into something she needed to expel.

The past was just a place where uncontrolled freaks you had never consciously decided to include in your life entered it anyway and staggered around, breaking things. Compared to the gentle, competent family she had chosen, they were monsters. Even someone like Linda, seemingly so warm and lively, was an unknown. Though Karen had felt happy and connected after talking to her, when she reflected on their conversation she realized that they had spoken mostly about Linda herself, mostly in glowing terms, without learning anything concrete about her that would make her real. Since graduating from college, since getting engaged and then married, since moving to this new, worse city, Karen had always mourned her growing isolation. She had longed for the unpredictable, haphazard quality that other people had, which she had found beautiful. What seemed more beautiful to her, now, was the new being, unsullied, perfect for now in every way, whose entire existence so far had unfolded under her gaze. Even if Karen was no longer connected to the chain of exhausting events that comprised her past, she could still attach herself to a whole life, pure and complete, in the form of her innocent, silent daughter. Her daughter would live whole inside her mind, inside her memory, forever.

As she rounded the corner to the block where she would find the café, Karen saw that something had gone on. In the vivid blue dusk, swaths of a brighter blue alternated with hot red, electrifying the trunks of trees and sides of buildings.

A few people milled around, talking; others walked past as though everything were just as it should be. With a terrifying expression on her face, Karen ran with the ugly stroller, her feet festooned with Band-Aids, toward police cars up ahead.

As she came close, she saw, first, a policewoman with a short blond ponytail, then her partner, who had a notepad, and then a potbellied man explaining something to him with vigorous gestures. She saw the vehicles double-parked by the entrance to the café where the lights were on and the barista slid a rag along the counter. There was no sign of Linda, or of her garish pinks and greens: Linda was gone. The light was ending. And then, in the arms of a policeman, standing in the yellow sheet of light cast by the streetlamp that had just come on, she saw Lila, she saw her baby. She squirmed gently, held by a stranger. Linda had left her there, gone about her own business. With a shudder, Karen thought of the stranger's hands, the strange hot arms.

Inside the baby, something was taking shape. There were colors and planes, indistinct, as if viewed through a thick layer of water. There was dimness and cold, the unmoored perception of bright blue and red, flashing. The baby watched as her mother came toward her with a face full of terror. The two eyes large and wild, the mouth pouring. With her gentle mind, the baby took the face in and waited, waited as it sank slowly to the top of a pile of things without names, waited for the noisy world to become still once more. It was all collecting inside there, gathering like dust, building, building up, until someday there would be enough for some part to pierce the surface of her silence and gasp out a piece of what lay beneath.

Jellyfish

She was truly happy for the first time in her life, and it felt just like living in a small room painted all white, with windows looking out onto impenetrable forest. It didn't bother her when she had to walk past strangers unwashed in the middle of the day or when she forgot a newly bought bag of groceries on the subway seat. Crossing the street, she paused to look up at an airplane etching a thin white stroke in the sky and was nearly hit by a taxi. Though it had been over a year, she staggered through the world like one freshly bludgeoned by love.

Now they were at a resort hotel by the beach, though the beach was really a five-minute drive away. All they had here was a forty-foot strip of damp sand visible during lowest tide, and a staircase that led directly into the sea. Karen looked down at the blue water frothing against the last visible stair. The water had a mouthwash color, something usually achieved through dye, making everything look unreal, retouched, staged somehow. Seeing her own hands foregrounded against this blue filled her with the sensation of dreaming, in the moments just before you wake up. Off in the far distance fishing boats floated at the horizon line, the only indication that this country had a real economy of its own, separate from the all-inclusive resorts that lined this stretch of land, which resembled utopian communes but operated secretly under cutthroat capitalist principles.

The water was cool, and looked as clear as a glass of water: you could see shells strewn on the ocean floor. But the unusually hot weather had caused jellyfish to multiply unchecked. They populated the shallows, a slight distortion in the shifting, flashing patterns of sunlight on sand. Beachgoers descended the staircase to steep their bodies in the tropical blue, but once they got out into the sea they stopped, looking down and moving around nervously, a few steps to the left, then to the right. One woman was stuck in waist-deep water, crying, her face deeply pink. She kept wiping it with short, rough motions that looked like slaps. Over and over she turned back toward the staircase, but she was too far away. The man she had come with was several feet away, doing the breaststroke in tight circles. "You have to kick their heads," he shouted to her. "Kick them out of your way!"

Daniel had proposed to her that morning and she said yes in an instant. He went to take a shower. Karen had left the bungalow, identical to every other in the resort, and walked out into the swelter. It seemed strange to be apart from him in this moment, but it felt even stranger to wait for him there in the overly cold hotel room, trying vaguely to read a magazine while he washed each part of his body with scrupulous care. She expected the world to feel different now that she had achieved a new life state. Instead, it was deathly hot. Karen walked out to the railing and stared down into the sea. It looked beautiful enough, but the water was haunted. If you waited patiently and let your eyes adjust, it would come into focus: the faint pale outline of a jellyfish, like a ghost of the jellyfish you had seen on TV or in photographs, a bland white space waiting to be colored in.

"She stood there wailing. Every few minutes it got louder, then she'd shout out 'I'm so scared!' or 'They're everywhere!' He just swam around. At the end he picked her up and carried her out."

"I love how easy it is to pick people up when you're in the water," Dan said, tilting a small full glass of orange juice into his throat.

"What?" Karen asked.

"That's what we used to do when we went on family vacation. Once I was a teenager, my dad used to let me pick him up and carry him around the pool. He was a big guy then, that's when he was still training for marathons. It was hard to do, but it was still possible." Dan smiled and stabbed at his breakfast sausage. He had chosen this resort for its high ratings on decor.

"That sounds nice," Karen said, uncertain. Dan's plate contained a horrifying amount of meat from all different cultures and civilizations.

"It *was* nice. My mom would bring us all virgin daiquiris from the bar and we'd pretend they were getting us drunk. My dad and I would use them like lances and try to joust in the water."

"Daiquiris?" Karen asked, trying to picture it, the novelty straw pointed outward, weaponized.

"No," said Dan, "my mom and sister. They tried to make themselves perfectly rigid and narrow at the tip."

"Oh, I see," said Karen. Karen had never heard of a happy childhood like Dan's from any real person, but she had seen things like it on TV screens. When he told her about the sunny, lively experiences of his past, she often thought of them as synopses or, if there were many, montage. She tried to ask the questions that would make these stories take on mass. Was this while his mother was working in prison law, trying to stop the construction of new facilities? Were his lawyer parents troubled by their work, did it make his childhood less bright? Did his father regret training so hard when it was a marathon that had blown out his knee? She looked out the restaurant window at the perfect blue water full of stinging tentacles, then at the resort-goers crowding the omelet bar, several of them calling out their orders at once. Behind the counter, a boy no older than sixteen regarded the ingredients with terror as he cracked two eggs into a small white bowl. Karen prayed that he would not do something tragic like try to escape.

"The worst part of it," said Karen thoughtfully, "was how happy he was. I watched him paddle around, do handstands, splash in the water, while she wept twenty feet away. He might as well have been whistling jauntily."

"Who?" Dan asked, looking up.

"Nothing," she said.

Her own parents had not known how to vacation at all. Once a year, usually in the spring or summer, they would take Karen with them on a trip to someplace similar in climate and geography to the place in which they lived. When this happened, there was always a reason: to visit a great-aunt or a friend of a relative, or to go to one of her father's professional conferences, where archivists gathered to listen to panels on database administration. On these trips they stayed in motels or hotels some distance from the center of town, where diverse locations like Atlanta, Tallahassee, and Richmond converged in an interchangeable span of franchises and family restaurants. For years they ate the motel waffles and the croissants of the nicer hotel chains together, but since she graduated from college her parents had found a new joy in traveling without her, recreationally. Last year they traveled to Morocco and stayed in a converted inn that had once been a small summer palace. Attached to their mass travel e-mail, Karen found photos of her father looming over a bowl of dried apricots, his mouth exaggeratedly open in an expression of surprise. She found her mother grinning at a small tame falcon perched on her open hand. Her mother was wearing a huge straw hat encircled by small multicolored bells, a tourist hat. Her father had captioned the photo "my wife has all the bells & whistles!" Karen had the uncomfortable feeling that they had advanced, leaving her behind.

Dan went to the buffet for seconds, leaving behind a plate on which teriyaki chicken chunks abutted slices of smoked ham piled askew, stratified and resembling steep cliffs or canyons. The plate signaled great abundance and great waste at the same time, canceling itself out. Karen chewed at a massive piece of underripe cantaloupe and swallowed. The hard angles pressed against her inner throat, sliding. Karen thought to herself that she'd probably become a vegetarian, someday.

. . .

A few hours later, it was time to eat again: they ordered at their seats by the pool from a menu as thick as a book. Turning its huge plastic-covered pages made Karen feel like a child again, gaping at the pictures of odd-colored food shot too closely, curiously shiny. "No thank you," Karen said to the waiter who tried to fill her water glass. "Stay hydrated," Dan said, pushing his own glass over to her. It was too hot to move, and they sat by the pool with their laptops on, waiting for more food to come to them and be consumed. As the staff door swung open, Karen could hear several people laughing together in a language she did not understand.

Dan seemed to be working on an architecture project next to her, though he had promised that he would not bring any work along on their vacation. He stared into his screen at a contorted orange shape, zooming in and out on it, rotating it to one side or the other, sighing deeply. Meanwhile, Karen had become obsessed with reading about jellyfish. The Nomura jellyfish could grow up to two meters in diameter, and weigh up to 450 pounds. A ten-ton Japanese fishing boat had capsized after trying to haul up a load of Nomuras caught in the net. She stared at a photo of giant jellyfish clogging a water treatment plant, their heads like plastic bags full of dirty water. She clicked on one link and then back to the search screen to click on another and another. She learned with horror that a jellyfish stinger was not just a stinger: it was a sac of toxins that ruptured when touched, shooting out a ridged, wicked-looking spine. This structure, called a nematocyst, was intelligent—it knew the difference between random pressure and human skin.

In the drawings of the jellyfish nematocysts, the stingers resembled harpoons shooting into the flesh and burying themselves there, lodging like insect splinters below the surface. Karen suddenly felt like she was going to throw up.

"I'm going to cancel my order," she said to Dan, standing abruptly.

"What? Why?" he asked, looking up from his small virtual object.

"I'm not hungry," Karen said.

"Then why did you order?" he asked, exasperated.

"Because you wanted to! You decided!" Karen replied, mirroring his tone.

"I didn't decide anything," said Dan. "It's lunchtime. Time decided it."

"You always decide," Karen said more quietly, looking out at the sea.

Dan looked at her, then followed her gaze out to the water. A pair of kids floated offshore, clinging to a boogie board. At this distance it was impossible to see whether they were huddled in fear, or just talking. Karen sat back down.

"Cancel it," Dan said, "and you can eat later, when you're hungry."

Karen nodded and stood back up, looking for the waiter. When the waiter saw her, he disappeared for a moment and then walked toward them, carrying a large tray. He went to Dan's side and set down a beige-colored pad thai. Then he came around to Karen's and set down a large, puffy pizza. As Dan ate, Karen regarded her unwanted pizza. It had the shape and pattern of a pizza, but the cheese on top was creamy like brie, the tomato sauce had a deep burgundy color. It was as though somebody who had never known a pizza in real life had created one based on a vintage photograph and a dictionary entry. Several feet away, a family of French tourists sat drinking tall blue drinks and eating cheese sandwiches. The children played a game that involved slapping each other's hands; sharp smacks cut through the drowse of the waves and of buzzing insects.

When she first met Dan, a graduate school classmate of her friend Naomi, she had called him "fun," which was not the same thing as "exciting." Most of the people Karen dated had pushy personalities and visible insecurities: when she soothed their worries, it created a serene feeling in her, like petting a cat. When the two of them experienced worries simultaneously, huge fights would develop and last anywhere from one to three days. Dan's emotional life was sturdier: Karen admired how he shrugged off smaller offenses and articulated his disagreement with larger ones in simple, practical language. He had experienced few conflicts in his life, and those he remembered were strange to her. Once he told her about a graduate school rival, Paul Mitchell, who had stolen his idea for the semester's final project. They had been assigned to come up with a concept and suite of renderings for a public library proposed in downtown Los Angeles. Dan's idea had been an elegant oval with a large, open central space where patrons could gather and socialize, with stacks and quiet study spaces radiating outward. The building would have a natural "hearth" to it, and visitors could choose what type of "heat" they wanted to experience by placing themselves in relation to it.

Two days before his presentation, Paul had come to class

with the same building, identical down to the colors used and the key terms bolded on his slides. He looked straight at Dan while giving his talk, smirking. Dan ended up having to design an entirely new library, this time conceived as a honeycomb of adaptable nooks that could become spaces for private reading or cozy group interaction. In the end, his two-day project received the highest score in the class, he told her: the story ended there. But had he confronted Paul Mitchell afterward? Why was Paul so bent on fucking him over? Had Dan been angry, and if so, how did he exhibit it? Karen couldn't understand how these encounters had marked him, and she had always believed that a person without trauma was dangerous in some way, untested. Also bizarre: in all of his stories, Dan ended up succeeding.

The health and robustness of his mind were compelling to her: like an alien or a hero, she believed him capable of anything. At the same time, she felt useless in the face of his decisions, which she believed were stronger than her own. She didn't understand why he had arrived at the decision to propose to her today, rather than some day earlier or later. Now, as she watched him staring at his computer, outlined in sweat and brilliant sunshine, the air around them so hot that it almost seemed to wobble, Karen felt an urgent and acrimonious feeling rise in her.

"What's that?" Karen demanded, pointing to the ugly form on-screen.

"It's the first concept for a hybrid gallery-gym," Dan said. "Victor's firm got the commission, and he wants me to help out. He actually wants to offer me a job. I'm just trying to look at the idea and figure out what he's thinking." He spun the shape around casually. It slowed and settled on a slant, looking cheap.

"Where would the job be?" Karen asked. "Don't you think you should have told me?"

"Boston," said Dan. He looked at her. "But there isn't even an offer yet."

Karen stared into the shallow pool. Jellyfish are a gathering of protein, water, nerves—no brain. The bungalow they had paid for cost over two hundred American dollars a night, times four nights. They still had two nights to go. It was embarrassing to be here, seeing into the lives of so many strangers: for the first time, she missed the generic motels of her childhood, where people were kept safely stowed away from one another. She wished she had never seen the swimming couple, whose discord had ruined the morning's fragile new feeling.

"It's not a big deal," he said, reaching over and squeezing her arm.

"Don't you think," Karen said in a wavering voice, "that we should talk about the engagement?"

"Because of this?" Dan asked. His voice was flattening, the way it did when he was angry. "Are you serious?"

Karen spoke carefully, in clipped phrases. "I mean, it just happened this morning. Why aren't we talking about it? Why aren't we happy? Shouldn't it change this whole day? Make it better? Shouldn't it be present in everything we say or do?"

"I'm having a great day," he replied stiffly. "Aren't you?"

She stared at him reproachfully.

"This is ridiculous," Dan said.

Karen felt confused and angry. She was only trying to communicate, and she felt that nothing should be off-limits on the day of their engagement. If anything, she wanted to delve more deeply into their relationship, learn about it, immerse herself.

"You know what," Dan said, standing up. "Let's take an hour to cool off. I'll be in the room. You can find me whenever you want."

As he walked off toward the rows of indistinguishable cottages, their shapes modern but boring, Karen tried not to cry. Alone among vacationers, she closed her eyes and tried to will away the people around her, playing, laughing, sucking drinks through convoluted plastic straws. With her eyes closed, their presence only grew louder: she could hear mouths squishing around bread, mucus unclogging deep within a head. The ocean sound was everywhere, close and encroaching, coming to carry her away. Then, at some point, she was asleep.

She awoke to the sensation of a damp towel being draped over her face, one was already on her torso. It felt like a funeral ritual, gently conducted. She pulled the towel away and blinked into the impossibly bright light. The ocean had come up almost to the railing: now it was only a few feet of tile that separated her from the sea and everything in it. To her right stood a man about her age, wearing navy blue shorts and a black T-shirt, some outfit that said nothing about who he was. He had picked up the towel she had thrown on the ground and was holding it out to her.

"You're burning," he said flatly, in a completely normal

American voice. He looked at her expressionlessly, waiting. He was dramatically handsome.

Karen reached for the towel, pressed it against her face. There was an insistent feeling on the surface of her skin, like her face was falling asleep and blushing at the same time. She felt thirsty, or maybe faint.

"Thank you," she muttered. She looked around. The French family was gone, and so were the sunbathers strewn on the hurricane wall. It seemed shameful to sleep out here, in public. Karen thought of someone, a strange man or woman, watching her unconscious face, her slack, open mouth. The sun was in a different place now, but it was no cooler than before.

"It's okay. People here do this all the time," he said, gesturing at his own face. Karen supposed he meant getting as sunburned as she must be right now.

"Well, thank you," she said. "I usually pay more attention." She lay stiffly beneath the towel he had placed on top of her body. "Have you been at this place for a while?"

The man nodded. "Years," he said.

Karen didn't know whether he was joking, so she laughed uncomfortably.

"I work here," he explained. "I'm the director of culinary services."

"Oh, wow," Karen said. "How did you end up here?" Though he seemed strange—stiff, or boring—she was glad for the distraction of talking to him. There was no place on this resort for her anymore: the sun, the water, and her fiancé had all turned against her.

"Well," he said, "I'm a world traveler. That's the first

thing. I've been all over the world, and I've tried everything they have to offer, in terms of food." He grew more and more animated as he talked about himself. "You name it. I've eaten live squid in Tokyo-cho and fresh chicharróns in Mexico City. I have a good handle on what's authentic, and how to achieve it. So when my buddy came to me and said he didn't need a chef, he needed someone to run the chefs, I put my hand up."

Karen glanced at the lamentable pizza she had ordered, whole and wet-looking on the table to her left.

"Plus, to live in a gorgeous place," he added, "like all of this." He held his arms out in front of him, palms up, gazing into the bungalow village.

"It is very beautiful," Karen said, though she wasn't sure. Each bungalow had an identical porch with a gate on the right or left side. Each bungalow had a small, intensely groomed tree blooming with fragrant white flowers and a small kidney-shaped pond populated by frogs that you sometimes saw dead on the path, crushed by feet. The effect of so many small, identical details multiplied and extended into the far distance was nightmarish, an optical illusion made suffocatingly real. She imagined herself running forever into the far distance and remaining somehow in the same place.

"You have *no* idea," he said, deeply emphasizing the word *no*.

"I just wish," she said, "that it was safe to swim. I've never seen so many jellyfish at once."

He nodded deeply. "They're responding to the critical upheaval in the climate. The jelly blooms are destroying us. Not only that, but we lose beach every season to erosion, and storms." Little creases formed at the outer corners of his eyes: he seemed genuinely troubled.

"I was watching one couple this morning," Karen said, looking up at his face. "His girlfriend was bawling for maybe thirty minutes straight. She was terrified of them, the jellyfish. He just swam around, having a great time."

"That's ice-cold," he replied, shaking his head firmly. He looked off toward the horizon line, where a yacht cut through gray haze. Karen smiled up at him.

"You know," he said suddenly, looking down at her, "I know some bloom-free beaches. It's a lot better farther down the coast. Different currents, colder ones—the ones the surfers chase."

"Oh wow," said Karen.

"It's maybe ten or fifteen minutes away, if you have wheels." He shrugged. "I could give you a ride."

Karen looked down at her stinging, reddening arms. If she went back to the room, would she find Dan angry with her still, fiddling with shapes and abstractions? When she saw him, would she feel relief or just a return of that rigid feeling? From the long, flat rectangle of the shallow resort pool she could see the man-made water close by, empty and painted blue, and the wild water farther off. This handsome man with the convincing feelings seemed benign. Just because he was attractive didn't make him dishonest: it could even turn out to be the case that his attractiveness had made him more honest than other people since he hadn't had to lie to get what he wanted. It was then that she realized, like an epiphany, that all the employees around her were significantly more attractive than the average guest. But what was the strategy behind this hiring practice? Was it to make the guests feel young and attractive too? To make guests feel that this was a beautiful and clean place? Or to show the resort's power and high standing, as evidenced by its ability to recruit such good-looking people from the towns nearby, people who conceivably had more opportunities than average? Karen felt a headache coming on. The director of culinary services looked impatient as he stood before her, watching her make up her mind.

"Are you going now?" she asked, not sure how his answer would affect her decision.

"If you're ready," he replied, looking her up and down as if for the first time.

Karen thought of the cold, tense bungalow, set behind the eerie pond and tree. "Okay," she said, turning to grab her bag.

"Hold on," he said, a little sternly. Karen froze. He pointed at the terrible pizza, still perfectly intact. "Don't you want to get that boxed up?"

"Oh, right," Karen said. She walked to the bar and asked for a box. She walked back to the table and began the process of shoving the terrible pizza into the too-small Styrofoam container. It fit: folded over twice, with a chunk of crust torn off.

"Great," he said.

His name was EJ, and the vehicle he owned was an old motorbike painted construction-cone orange. The rattle of its worn-down motor clashed alarmingly with the deep, serene green of the jungle around them. When EJ slowed down to avoid potholes or clear a curve, the engine sputtered a deeply unwholesome gray smoke.

"I'm Karen," Karen said, shouting into the rush of air.

"What?" EJ shouted. "I can't hear you!"

The groves of palm trees and bananas were a broad smudge around them, as EJ made alarming decisions about when to barrel through piles of palm debris and when to swerve suddenly, wrenching around them. Absolute time and absolute speed were difficult to gauge on a motorbike, Karen thought as she tried to cling to EJ's sweat-soaked back without digging her fingernails into the flesh, but it seemed as though they could die on this ride. In her left hand, she clutched the Styrofoam box packed with awful pizza: she would have dropped it, but it was still possible that EJ would turn the bike around and make them go back for it.

"Where is it?" she shouted.

"Soon!" he shouted back. "Can you try to sit still?" They were both visibly annoyed, and annoyed with the other person for showing it. Each time she shifted on her piece of the seat, EJ let out a grunt and made a big show of correcting for the wobble Karen had created as she struggled to rebalance herself.

"Stop wiggling around!" he shouted over his shoulder.

"What?" Karen shouted back.

Out of nowhere, EJ made a sharp left turn onto a dirt road. Gravel crackled beneath motorbike wheels as they barreled down the narrowing path. And then, abruptly, the ocean splayed out before them, gray-blue in the deteriorated

light, more real and less pretty than the toothpaste water
the resort was built to exploit. EJ dismounted and kicked
his thong sandals off in the sand. "Holy shit," he said, "glad
that's over!" He did a couple cursory stretches of his ham-
strings and went into a downward dog. Now it was like
Karen wasn't even there: he pulled off his shirt and jogged
toward the water with an easy stride. From time to time,
she saw him punch at the air with his right fist in a gesture
of triumph.

Karen walked slowly up to the water. She had no idea
whether she was supposed to follow him in, but she didn't
care. EJ was only a fleck in the distance at this point, bobbing among waves. If she squinted her eyes into the shifting
surface she could see the notion of his head or arm or leg
as he swam around in the deeper water, among the cold
currents or other such bullshit. She set the Styrofoam box
down on the sand, dropped her tote bag. She slid off her sandals and piled some sand onto them, so they wouldn't blow
away: Dan had taught her to do this, last summer at Fort
Tilden. She walked into the sea gingerly, step by step, the
water lukewarm and smelling of brine and tar. Once when
she was eighteen she had done something like this: she let
an art professor from the college next to her own drive her
in his car to a beach she didn't even know the name of. He
wore a black, full-body wetsuit; she had walked waist-deep
into the waves fully clothed. As he dove and surfaced like
a seal in the clear water, she had realized that she knew
almost nothing about him. She had looked down at her skirt
swirling around the dim, disappearing legs and hoped that
she'd make it back to the car, back to town, to live free of

mistakes like this one. And now, almost a decade later, she had made the exact same mistake.

Knee-deep in the surf, Karen willed herself to take another step, and another. She would move to Boston if she had to. She would get back to the bungalow, somehow, and she would say all of this to Dan: they had made the right decision, she was happy, she was ready to become even happier. Waist-deep in the warm gray water, she saw something wobbling beneath the surface. It was Styrofoam-white and resembled a piece of trash, suspended between the surface and the sand. She looked to her left, to her right. As she stared into the water, the floating shapes came into view all at once: like constellations they were there, venomous and drifting, more numerous than she could even have imagined.

In the summer between high school and college, Karen's father was diagnosed with cancer. The cancer was malignant, but not incurable. Curing it would, however, involve a great deal of pain: the pain of incision, extraction, and then days of radiation battering the flesh invisibly. Her father underwent the course of treatment almost without comment, so that the only visible trace of its effect was his body lying on the couch for most of each day, silently watching baseball on a dizzyingly colorful TV screen. That summer, Karen stayed away from the house as much as possible. She walked for hours around their town and the banks of the creek, picking up pebbles and putting them in her pockets, emptying them out someplace different but equivalent. And when she came home for dinner she joined her parents in choosing not to speak about the cancer, though it wasn't clear what else there was to speak about.

Even while it was happening, she sensed that she was living in disaster and failing to make herself adequate to the situation. What she wanted to say to her mother and father she couldn't say, what she wanted to ignore she couldn't ignore. After the remission, Karen promised herself that she would be ready for the next true disaster, she would identify it and react appropriately. She was haunted by the feeling that, even though her father had lived, she had let him die.

Since then, Karen had looked for disaster at every step in her life, but had discovered that each disaster she thought she had discovered was inadequate to the concept. This walk home, alone, on an unlit foreign road lined by deep, rock-filled gutters could end up being a true disaster—but it unfolded so slowly, so ponderously, and out there on the dangerous peaceful street the air smelled ecstatically of blooming plumeria. There were no clear signs to react to: peril was everywhere, intermingled with the mundane. Karen felt that all her life she would be moving from positions of perceived danger to positions of perceived safety without ever knowing which impressions were correct. And as she had this thought, her mood abruptly inverted: now she was feeling relief, joy, even something close to euphoria. Inhuman calls echoed through the vegetal thick; a siren went off far away.

On a road like this one, with no shoulder and no speed limit, any car that came along could hit her. If she was on the right road, she wouldn't be back at the bungalow for hours. Poisonous animals lived in this area—snakes, scorpions, centipedes. The moon was large and bright over-head, and smooth like a stone. She didn't know what she'd tell Dan when she got back to him, but she knew he'd be there, passed out on the bed with his laptop still open and his teeth unbrushed. He'd have fallen asleep believing she'd be back soon. On the table there'd be some cake or a cookie as an apology for whatever had happened by the pool that afternoon. And on her nightstand, there'd be a fresh glass of water.

Intimation

I was trying to think of all the different things I liked about doors. Their size, their heft, the sense that they were made for bodies to pass through them freely. The way they put holes in spaces in which you would otherwise be trapped forever, looking for some way in or out. All of the best moments in my life had been preceded by entering or exiting a door, or maybe just having a door waiting there in the background, offering the possibility of escape. They were the only things I could think of that were truly reversible: no clear beginning or ending, passing endlessly through a series of midpoints and temporary stops. They were beautiful in this revocability, flexible and soft.

All except this door, which seemed to be unidirectional.

From the outer side it had looked like any other, but here I was running my hands over it and looking for the seam, clawing at it, pounding my hands against this faint echo of a door that lacked all the features I had heretofore prized among its kind. The doorknob was fixed in place, and when I ran my fingers over the line, it felt of paint, thick and dark, on a smooth surface. If this door offered hope, it was only in trompe l'oeil form, a thin veneer of it laid planlessly. I turned to look for another way out.

Behind me lay the insides of a small house: coffee table, sofa, then a dining table and chairs. What looked like a kitchen to the right, then a long, narrow hallway that probably ended in a bedroom or bathroom. The apartment was small, and it seemed to funnel off into a point too small for anyone to step into, or out from. A man was seated on the sofa. He watched me, and he tilted his head.

What are you looking for? he said.

What's wrong with this door? I said.

That's a really strange question, he responded.

Something about his statement really irritated me. Yes, I was able to see how it could be considered a strange question. But in this situation, this strange situation, it seemed to be the only reasonable question to have. The fact that he wasn't asking the question himself made him the strangest element here. At least by the standards that existed outside this house.

Look, sorry, where are my manners? he said. Have a seat, would you like anything?

I had just walked into his house, a complete stranger, and began clawing at the walls, tearing at the empty form of the door painted on it. I wanted him to feel as I did, trapped and hungry for answers. He should have been demanding information from me, demanding to know why I was here and who I was.

Don't you want to know how I got in here? I asked.

He laughed a little. Okay, he replied, I'll bite. How did you get in here?

I'm not sure, I said.

Now that we've settled that, he said tolerantly, do you or do you not want something to eat? A beverage? He stood up and headed over to the dining table.

I used to have a pet mouse that was actually just a normal mouse that had been living in our kitchen, someplace behind the oven. My mother caught it in a Havahart one weekend and I begged her to give it to me instead of crushing its head with a hammer and flushing it down the toilet, as she had threatened repeatedly to do. This mouse was cute, but it never got used to the fact that it now lived in a cage. It smelled bad in a feral way and wouldn't learn to groom itself. You couldn't play with it because it was wild, dirty, and fierce, but I used to like to press my face up to the clear plastic walls of its habitat and watch it digging furiously at the bounds, and when I did this I tried to make sure that my face showed a similarly desperate expression just so the mouse would know that it wasn't crazy.

. . .

He was pouring a glass of wine and didn't seem to be looking at me at all.

You have beautiful eyes, he said all of a sudden.

I hated compliments like that, compliments that carved out one particular part of your body and put it on a platter for viewing. It always took a while for me to reabsorb that body part afterward, to add it back to the whole. The best kind of compliment to give me was something vague, plausible. You're all right. Or, Don't worry, it gets better.

Eh, I replied.

He handed me the glass and began saying things to me. He described his feelings on organized religion and organized sports, on organizations in general, on bodily organs (the liver was his favorite and, he felt, often overlooked), and the economics of organic fruits and vegetables. I felt invaded at first, but as he talked, I experienced a sudden swell of something calmer, more complacent. This was a feeling that he talked into me; it sank in through the skin. It wasn't anything in particular he had said, just the fact that he kept saying it, whether I responded or not. This ceaseless stream of talk might seem aggressive from some perspectives, something I couldn't affect except through participation, but I felt it more like light illuminating a room, a harsh and inescapable substance that was ultimately harmless.

• • •

This feeling of lessening disturbance, coming from within myself, unexpected, was profoundly disturbing. As I sat still, growing less and less alarmed by the situation, I knew that I had to move fast, move as fast and as far as I could within this small, cramped house.

Do you have a bathroom here that I could use? I asked.

You don't need to go to the bathroom, he said. He said it like it was a fact that he had read recently, in some news article. And it was true: nothing had changed for me physically since I entered this house. I had grown no thirstier or hungrier, though my mental parts felt increasingly in flux.

What I mean to say is, I have to go into the other room by myself, I said.

For what reason? he asked.

I couldn't think of a good answer. I couldn't tell him that I was going to look for a functional door or window that I could sneak out of without seeming ungrateful for his hospitality. I couldn't think of a way to tell him that I wanted to get away without sounding crazy, like a person not in command of her own life choices. I couldn't think of anything at all, really: it was so warm in here, so much warmer than it had been outside, and the air seemed a bit thicker and sweeter than usual, like watered-down honey.

. . .

I'm going to bake a cake? I said, testing this answer out.

Well, that sounds great, maybe we'll have something to celebrate in the future, he said, winking in my general direction.

I left the room before I could figure out exactly what bothered me about his response. Was it the way it seemed to
assume a future for the two of us? A future in which I would
continue to be unable to leave this house? Was it the pre-
sumption that I was making a cake for him when, really, I
had no idea why I was making a cake at all?

Now I was in the kitchen and I could at least rely on the
task to keep me from thinking of those questions. I took
cocoa, sugar, flour, salt, baking powder, vanilla extract, and
butter from the various storage places of the kitchen. What
was strange was that all of these things were present in the
room, everything I needed, but nothing else. The fridge
contained one stick of butter and four eggs, no more. The
cabinets were empty except for the dry ingredients of my
cake, exactly one cake's worth. This information seemed to
have a bearing on my situation, and I filed it away to think
about it later.

Ever since I was young, I had maintained a special agree-
ment with myself wherein I was permitted to avoid thinking about whatever I wished, at that moment, to avoid
thinking about, provided that I think instead about another

problem that I had wished to avoid thinking about in the past. In this way, I would never be shirking my responsibilities entirely, but I also would not have to deal with the most difficult of the possible problems at its most pressing time. At this moment, I decided that I would try thinking about the problem of reversibility and irreversibility in physical processes. Why was it true that one could stir sugar into a cup of tea, but not stir it back out? Why did living things age only in one direction, and so unfalteringly in that direction, without pauses or stops?

By exerting my own energy, I was able to combine the ingredients of this cake together in the mixing bowl. This was done freely, of my own will. Why, then, could no amount of effort or will unmix the ingredients, make them as they were before, whole and full of potential? If I could unmake this cake as neatly as I could make it, I would be able to stay here in this separate room forever, making and unmaking and never having to deal with the man in the first room who seemed to have ideas about me that I didn't share.

It was at this moment that I realized I had forgotten the baking soda, and without it I knew the cake would turn out wrong, though I did not know in what way, exactly.

I went back into the living room to ask him if he had any baking soda in some nook I hadn't checked, but when I entered the room I saw him hiding something under the dining table.

. . .

What's that? I asked.

What are you doing, trying to ruin the surprise? he responded.

I would have asked about the surprise, but I knew it would go nowhere or go somewhere I didn't want to go. So I asked, instead, about the baking soda. He looked uneasy.

You should have everything there that you need, he said. Maybe you got the recipe wrong, he added.

I looked angry, and then I picked up one of the plates and smashed it on the floor.

It seemed as though, being the only two people in this small, closed-in space, we couldn't help but have a relationship, and if we couldn't help but have a relationship, I felt that it was important to be upset now so that he would not shift the blame to me in the future.

Suddenly he also looked angry, and he picked up a larger plate and smashed it near mine.

We stood there, pieces of plate scattering the ground between us. Then he spoke.

Sorry, he said.

. . .

There was nothing else I could do but say sorry myself. His apology had left a residue in me, a residue on my thinking, and continuing on in this house without saying it would be entirely awkward. It would turn the small space toxic. So I said it, though I tried to lessen the potency of the apology by mumbling.

I have something to ask you, he said.

I shifted my position to one more suitable for being asked a question. I was now curled up on the couch with my knees pressed up against my body, my knees shielding my face from seeing what was going on.

My question is, he began. I think I knew from the first time I met you that I would not be meeting another person quite like you ever again. You are unlike anyone else around here. I have not seen anyone like you in quite a while. So, should we be exclusive?

Everything seemed to be moving so fast. I had to stall.

When did we meet again? I asked.

It feels like forever ago, he said.

Wouldn't you say that this is still part of the first time that we've met? I asked.

. . .

He shrugged. You're being avoidant, he said. You probably have a history of it, he said.

I got up to go back to the kitchen and put the cake in the oven. Probably it would not go well for the cake, or for who-ever tried to eat the cake. It did not look as though the cake was going to turn out particularly nice, having been made for confusing reasons and lacking certain essential ingredi-ents. But what else was there to do? Wasn't a terrible cake better than some terrible cake batter?

What I really wanted was to opt out of the causal relation be-tween myself and this cake, the causal relation that I couldn't seem to avoid, living in this house that I now appeared to live in. The proximity was changing me: I couldn't avoid seeing or noticing things that happened in this place, and because I was the only other person around, things couldn't help but involve themselves in me. I decided to think about the orbital motions of the moon around the earth, and of what might happen if the force of one on the other ever ex-ceeded expectations, pulling the two uncomfortably close, causing them to crash together in a fiery and highly destruc-tive event. But he was taking up so much space in me now, I could no longer think around him, peer around him to the shapes of things I had known before I entered this place. What had he meant by a surprise, and what had he meant by something to celebrate? How much time had elapsed in his experience, and was it really different from how much time had elapsed in mine? Or was I instead just a highly avoidant person with serious difficulties connecting to others? I didn't want to be so difficult, but that difficulty felt like a part of me, a part that I didn't want taken over by new features belonging to a me that did not yet exist.

I heated the oven to 350 degrees. In this house events seemed to move unusually quickly. Would the cake still require the usual twenty-five to thirty minutes of baking? Or should I try to calculate the temporal properties of this home and scale the time appropriately?

I slid the cake into the oven and walked back into the room. I missed you, he said.

I missed you too, I said.

That sentence came as a real shock. It felt as though it were spoken from some point farther down my throat than tooth or tongue or gag reflex. It felt as though it came from someplace deep within my body, from some speech organ that I had never heard of, that had never been discovered, and that probably didn't actually exist at all.

He smiled warmly and took my hand. It felt strange at first, both colder and softer than I had expected. But when I reexamined that feeling, I found that I couldn't remember ever having expected something else.

Now we were standing around holding hands and not much was going on. I began to think of words I had known, just for fun, just to fill up the blank space in my head. Couch, I thought. Cuisinart, I thought.

The words felt different right now than they had before. They meant a little less, held a little less, but seemed somehow fuller: I had never really noticed how much sound there was in a word. The way it filled your mouth up with emptiness, a sort of loosened emptiness that you could tongue, an emptiness you could suck on like a stone. Stomach, I thought. Variety, I thought. Expectation. Intimation. Infiltration. Infiltration: I tongued that one further. I knew it had a hostile aspect, like someone breaking into your house or posing as someone that you should trust. But it also had a lovely sound, a kind of tapered point and a gently ruffled edge, and as I repeated it over and over in my mouth it took on a really great flavor and I thought of water filtering in and out of a piece of fabric, back and forth, moving between, soaking it and washing out, soaking in and taking with it pale tremors of color, memory, resistance, all that stuff, until I felt like one of those pieces of cloth on the television commercials that got washed with the name-brand cleanser and is now not only white, but silky and mountain-scented.

Suddenly, I remembered the cake.

I think I have to get the cake out of the oven, I told him. Hurry back, he said.

I walked across the room to the kitchen and I hoped that the cake would be okay. Certainly it wouldn't be pretty, but hopefully it would taste like something full of butter, sugar, and cocoa, which was what it was, and how bad could that be?

In the kitchen I took the cake out of the oven with two nice new oven mitts and I carried it back over to the dining-room table. As I set it down, I noticed something written on the top in pale blue icing.

Congratulations? I read.

Congratulations for what? I asked him.

It's your surprise, he replied. I had a very strange feeling in my stomach.

He advanced toward me holding something in his arms. As he got closer, I saw that it had a face. Look who it is, he said, smiling down at me.

Who is it? I asked.

Can't you tell? he replied.

I looked at it. It was a decent-size baby. It didn't look like a newborn. It didn't look like a toddler. I couldn't tell if it looked like me. I suppose we looked similar insofar as we were both humans, with eyes and noses in the right places. But at this stage, it was too difficult to say whether we resembled each other.

Why don't you hold it? he said. He levered it off into my arms.

I don't know, I said.

Just then it began to wail, and he handed me a little spoon full of mush.

Somehow I knew that if I put this food into the mouth of the baby, I would never be allowed to leave this house. But if I didn't put the food into the baby, who would? He wouldn't do it, and the baby was unlikely to feed itself until it was at least a week or so older. My best hope was to wait around, try to figure out how things happened here, and learn how to make time pass faster and faster until it was grown up and ready to leave. Then maybe I could sneak out through the hole it made as it escaped.

Say something to it, he said.

As I looked at the baby, I felt nothing taking shape in mind or mouth. I had no idea what the sort of things were that somebody would say to a baby. I had no idea why anyone would say anything to a baby. I held it carefully, as one would a sack of apples. And then, with him watching me, nodding encouragingly, I began to say to it, for lack of anything else to say, all the words I had ever known, in order.

III.

Fake Blood

It was some sort of banquet hall or ballroom, windowless and arrayed with candles, and containing thirty or forty people who turned toward me, staring. They stared at me as though they hoped they could fix me through staring, or at least stare me away. I felt a stickiness move across my skin, and because I could not shut their eyes, I shut my own.

When I opened them, I was still standing in a large room with many other people. Nothing in the situation had changed or would change, however much I wished for it, and that seemed unbearable in a way that I supposed I would be bearing anyhow. There were small, delicate cakes and little heaps of berries. There were balloons floating up against the ceiling and wilting on the ground, colored shapes lying still in the dim and festive light.

I had arrived in costume, but it was not a costume party. Just a normal party, they said.

I looked down at my body as if for the first time. It seemed impossible to get an accurate view of myself without a mirror or camera, something on the outside to look in. From the perspective of my eyes, my shoulders and torso were huge. My legs began in knees, short and stubby, then suddenly there were shoes and it was all done. I was dressed entirely in white: a short white vinyl dress and white stockings; short white gloves and white heels. I had on a hat with a red cross at the front, and I was covered in fake blood.

I had come dressed as a sexy nurse: the blood was mostly incidental, mostly a way to keep from getting mixed up with the other sexy nurses that inevitably turn up at costume parties. But this was a normal party, and as such the blood was now a real liability. It was perhaps the one factor that made it truly unimaginable for me to blend in with the elegant people that fluttered around nearby, laughing lightly and staring at me like I was covered in blood, which I was.

"Is there someplace I could stow my coat?" I asked.

The thing was to behave as normally as possible, more normally than was possible, in order to balance out the blood. All the attention in the room was pooling at my feet, and I needed something big and alarming to draw it away from me, or conversely, something very ordinary to mask it. I went over to the table to find something to hold in my hands. Empty plastic cups measured out the emptiness in neat rows, waiting to be filled or moved or restacked. These objects were pieces, building up toward a whole I could not at all recognize.

"A little bit of detergent and ammonia, that's what I would use," said a woman's voice from behind me, whispered harshly. It appeared some people were having trouble telling the fake blood from real, and this might account for the coagulation of fear in the space surrounding me. I mixed alcohol, juice, and ice until it approximated the right color, and then I tried to figure out a way to stand. The light was strange in there, and it seemed conceivable that I could find a place and position that would render the bloodstains invisible, camouflaged, like a dappled shadow falling on the surface of grass.

But my movements in and out of the shadowy areas of the room, covered in blood as I was, made the other party-goers nervous. My dress gave off a loud and plasticky sound when I shifted even slightly, and there was the tendency of my costume toward drippage. The other guests hunched in toward one another as I wriggled in the corners, trying to cancel out the stains. "You just can't hide something like that," a man's voice said with audible disgust, coming from someplace I was unable to see.

The way things were, all I could do was make the situation worse.

There are times when any amount of being within the world is like rubbing bare skin against sandpaper, when any form of motion is a kind of abrasion, leaving you raw and pink and vulnerable to the next thing. At these times, I prefer to close my eyes and be still, still like the cups or candles or crackers on the table, nerveless and open. I closed my eyes and tried to think of the thing furthest from my situation. I imagined a meadow and I populated it with sunlight, a small and rustic fence trailing toward the horizon, a little family of ducks and a couple of grazing sheep, a green and verdant field studded with small white flowers, possibly clover blossoms. But before I knew it, blood was everywhere, though the sheep continued to munch along idyllically, tearing at the reddened tufts with small, calm movements and very white teeth.

When I opened my eyes, a man was standing next to me, watching me with curiosity, mostly. There was a shyness to his staring that I found bearable, if only in contrast to the other forms of staring that were going on around and at me. "Hello," he said. "Hi," I responded. "My name's Andrew," he said.

I nodded. Where was all this going?

"Well, I wanted to tell you first off that your fake blood looks great. Really realistic. Really scary, you know? But without being actually too scary. Really great."

I was flattered by his eye for detail: in fact I had spent a good amount of time getting the blood right, perfecting the proportions and cooking times as I made it from scratch. My recipe was a variant on the classic Karo syrup and red food coloring used in horror movies from the 1980s. Six pints of Karo syrup at room temperature, three ounces of red food coloring, nondairy creamer for opacity, arrowroot powder for texture, blue food coloring for depth, a bit of honey for the complexion, and vanilla extract to improve the scent. As with real blood, every element of the fake served a vital purpose.

It looked like Andrew had something else he wanted to say.

"Well, I don't mean to bother you. I guess I just noticed you standing by yourself and I just was wondering. I mean, you don't have to answer. But I was wondering. Are you part of the murder mystery, too?"

"Murder mystery?" I asked.

"Yeah, the one in the other room. In the kitchen or whatever. The guy with the ax in him."

"I'm not part of any murder mystery," I explained. "I just made a mistake."

A woman's voice came from my right. "Murder mystery?" it said. "Oh, how fun!"

I turned and looked at her.

"Well," she said, directing herself toward Andrew and avoiding my glare, "let's have a look! It's about time something interesting happened here."

The other room was a dining room, smaller and more intimate than the large hall we had been in before, but similarly windowless and dim. Objects were overturned on the table and floor in a way that suggested a struggle, but one that had been carefully choreographed. The candelabras and vases lay on their sides, gently, and long-stemmed roses were strewn evenly across the room with an executioner's precision. On the ground under some of the roses was a man sprawled flat on his front, his face buried in the carpet and a large ax sticking up from the middle— the exact middle—of his back. A dark red substance pooled beneath his body.

Impressed sounds came from all around me.

"It's very realistic, don't you think?" "Looks very much like a murder." "John really went all out this year, that's for sure!" Who was John, and why was he letting this happen? And then: Who was this man, and was he in on the joke or was he, like me, waiting it out, hoping that everyone would find something else to stare at?

In the lower center of my body, two feelings were swirling together. On the one hand, the scene was too grisly to be real, and I sensed my fists relaxing, going loose. On the other, I had never seen this much blood before, real or fake, and what did I know? It might be exactly grisly enough to be real.

"Are we very sure he's not really dead?" I asked.

A tall man in a gray suit strode over and stuck a finger in the red puddle. He rubbed the substance between his finger and thumb, sniffed it briefly, and declared, "Corn syrup. Definitely corn syrup, you can tell from the texture: slippery, thick, and sticky as hell. Smells sweet, too. I think our hosts are probably having a good laugh at our expense! The looks on our faces!"

I was still uneasy, but the unease was lifting slowly. The man looked competent, like a doctor. Or like someone who could have gotten into medical school. And then I wanted so badly to let it all be normal: for the first time that night, nobody seemed bothered by me. They hardly seemed to notice, they were so busy marveling at the accuracy of the carnage, dipping their fingers in the spreading liquid and playfully terrorizing their dates. I looked over at Andrew, and when he smiled at me I smiled back.

Just then there was a scream, followed by another scream, followed by nervous laughter.

The man who had identified the blood as corn syrup was facedown on the floor, surrounded by women who alternated between laughing tightly and murmuring quietly to each other. In the middle of his back was an ax much like the ax stuck in the first man, though with a different manufacturer's name on its handle.

"Um," I said. "What just happened?"

Nobody knew. One moment he had been upright; the

next he was prostrate, and axed. Everyone agreed it was great showmanship. Some began to talk about how diffi-cult it would be to remove the stains from the plush beige carpet, how much it would cost.

"So, um," Andrew said, turning back toward me. "What sort of work do you do?"

I was a secretary, but also there on the rug the same dark substance was blossoming out from under the second axed man, and something about this bothered me immensely. I would never have considered myself an expert on real blood or murder mysteries or staged deaths or party etiquette, but I had a good deal of experience with fake blood; and this just did not look like genuine fake blood. There was a live-ness to its flow, and it filled the room with a dark and inde-finable scent.

"Andrew," I said. "I just don't feel comfortable with this."

He looked sad.

"I don't mean you. You've been very nice. But I'm worried about the guy with the ax. In him, I mean. The second one. It all happened so quickly. Don't you think we should check it again? Even if the first murder was staged, the second one could be real."

"Oh. That's a good idea," he said. He walked over and pulled the second ax out of the second man's back.

It looked pretty real.

"It looks pretty real," he said.

"But what does real look like?" I asked.

"Is anyone here a doctor?" Andrew asked, looking around the room. Nobody was a doctor, or if they were, they were not admitting to it. If I wanted to know whether this situation was normal or abnormal, I would have to be the one to do something; and of all possible situations, this was perhaps the only one that I was actually qualified to deal with. I took the ax from Andrew's grasp and touched the wet blade with a fingertip. I drew my hand away and touched the fingertip to my tongue, tasting metal.

"Oh, my god," I said. "This is not fake. We are all in terrible danger." I tried to say this in a way that was both urgent and calm, but when I saw all the people staring at me, I realized that I had made them only more suspicious of me, the one living person there who was also covered in blood. I looked over at Andrew, and he looked away.

Another scream came from behind me, and when I turned around the woman I had glared at just a few minutes earlier was on the floor, an ax in her back.

"We need to move to another room," I said.

The other guests reluctantly followed me back to the banquet hall. What to do now? From the dining room, another scream: I already knew what I'd find if I went back there, and I thought to myself that if we followed the rules, perhaps we'd all make it out fine. If we figured out the rules and then followed them. All around me people were beginning to panic, searching for exits.

As it turned out, there were no exits.

We pounded the walls and screamed, to no effect. Some guests went into hysterics, sobbing on the floor, until they realized that nothing at all was going to change. Then they stood, oddly calm. One man grabbed the hand of a woman. "I love you," he said, pulling her hand to his chest and pushing it up against his heart. "What's your name again?"

she asked. "Jonathan," he said, "and I love you." A pause. "Okay," she said. They clung to each other, balled up in a corner, and as they did, others started to confess things, as well. "I need you." "I always hated you, but right now I don't mind you." "Would you please hold my head in your hands? Just hold it, really grab it, and tell me everything's going to be okay? Please?" Soon everyone was huddled in corners, except Andrew and me. I tried not to look at him too directly. If these were in fact the last moments of my life, I did not want to spend them in embarrassment.

It seemed like so much had happened, but still nothing had changed. I was back in the banquet hall, covered in fake blood, feeling left out, and looking for something to hold. Andrew was in the middle of the room, watching me, and I closed my eyes and thought about the meadow. This time, I would keep the sheep clean and snowy white. I added a stream and a large oak tree, birds coming to rest in its boughs. It was afternoon there, late afternoon, growing later.

I heard a noise, and I opened my eyes. Andrew was down. Another ax.

The rules had changed: the banquet hall was no longer safe. And with Andrew gone, there was no longer any reason to stay.

"We have to move," I said loudly to the room. "We have to move on." The hall had only two doors: one led to the dining room, which was certainly unsafe, and one to the basement, which really seemed like a bad idea, but at least uncertainly so.

"I'm going to the basement," I said. "We can barricade

ourselves in there." Nobody else said anything. I looked at them all one last time, balled up in their respective corners, and walked down the stairs.

The basement was both larger and cozier than I had expected. The ceilings went high, and the fluorescent lights far above buzzed in a way that reminded me of the outdoors, the outdoors during warmer months, when the air and the ground seemed bright all over with the lives of insects and plants. The space was cavernous, but it was full: there were piles of objects all around me, large piles reaching ten, twelve, fifteen feet into the air. They looked like they had been collected and sorted by someone very patient, someone with a lot of time on his hands. Or her hands. There was a large heap of flannel shirts, mostly plaid. A pile of *Time* magazines. A pile of athletic equipment, mostly football helmets. Wedding dresses. Gerbil cages.

By the time I found the pile of bloodied nurse costumes, almost nothing would have surprised me. This one reached nearly to the ceiling, hundreds or thousands of white vinyl dresses crumpled and stacked, strewn and sprawled, covered in blood. White nurses' caps stuck out at odd angles, studding the heap with crisp red crosses.

I found the costumes and I felt, for the first time since this whole thing began, that I truly belonged somewhere. I could crawl into this mountain of white and red, I could hide in it until the danger passed, or at least until the danger came to find me. All the mistakes I had made this night, everything from my nurse outfit to the way I had left things with Andrew: all of it seemed justified, purposeful, in light of this gigantic pile of bloody clothing.

I eased myself in, with some struggle and much noise. The vinyl surrounding me squealed against the vinyl on my body, making a sound like a thousand balloons rubbing together at once. The center of the pile was dark, slippery, and wet with blood, either real or fake. I hardly noticed the distinction anymore: sweet or salty, warm or cold, it was all horrible, and I curled up in it.

I thought about the events upstairs, and who the killer might have been. I thought about Andrew and how nice he had been to me, and how incredibly, unbelievably nice he probably was to people who were dressed normally in normal situations where nobody feared or resented them. What had he been thinking right before he was axed? Had he been thinking about me?

It was horrible, like I said, lying like a dead nurse among a pile of bloody costumes. It was horrible, but at the same time it was not so bad. It was not so bad, and at the same time it was horrible. But there was a feeling building in me now that I hadn't felt since I'd shown up at this stupid party: I was excited. Something was going to happen. Either this would work, or it wouldn't. Either I would be spared, or I would die. Either death was something that could be fooled, outwitted, outplayed, or it was not. However things ended, I would learn something about the world in which, for the moment, I continued to live.

Hylomorphosis

*Because they have seen angels, and other divine numina, repre-
sented by painters with a certain splendour and light, and have
heard that these are spirits and are so called by theologians; so
that in consequence they think that the spirituous stuff in our
bodies must be similar.*

—JOHANNES ARGENTERIUS, *De Somno et Vigilia*, 1556

An angel faces the painting of the famous angel with sword
looming above a battle. Figure blurred out, scene blurred out.
The painted angel's face like a thumbprint, darkened by two
depressions, one above and one beneath. The difficulty with
describing an angel or its movements: they lack organs of
sense or motion. Their bodies defined by absence. The angel
facing the painting reaches up toward its own body. Its fingers
grope the tranquillity of that perfect head, smooth as a plate.
It finds the middle of its face and pushes in. The question is:
Can an angel become anything it has not already been?

———————

The mouths of an angel are threefold: With one, he breathes
of the pure and refined air of glorious realms, the light of God

filling his body with lightness. With the second, he eats of the meat of the spirit and drinks in long drafts the clear water of the soul, both of which make heavy the banquet of God, and are eternal and immune to spoilage. With the third, he utters words of truth, handed down to him from the highest order. In man, however, the functions threefold are merged in one organ, and hence his purposes and the ends to which he applies himself shall always be indistinct, unintelligible.

———————

The angels sit and weep. Just as suddenly, they stand and laugh. They are testing out their new-made mouths. The angels stick fingers in their mouths, one by one, and root around in them, scratching at the top, the soft yielding sides that bulge when tried. The angels scratch until they pierce membrane and nothing seeps through. The angels discover a funny sound made by squishing the cheeks in, then forward, so that the lips purse at the front in imitation of a fish. They lack respect for the bodily ideal, for its integrity and originary form. They heal before the wound can weep. The angels practice a self-mortification of such innocent clumsiness that it cannot carry any redemptive value: and, in any case, what have they to atone for? Virtue weighs upon them like a coat made of air.

———————

Suppose that archangel Gabriel intends to have cognition of his fellow angel Raphael, but also of human beings, trees, and other things in the material world. To do so, he cannot simply observe or encounter the objects aforementioned: without organs of sense or action, he must instead adopt his habit, a habit unique and individual, the fulfillment of which shall grant access to all things simultaneously, in their essence. In this manner, a knowledge perfect and unequivocal is achieved without returning to the problem of access, which is an issue only for beings of bounded material.

———

1. The mouths of angels are soft and sweet: Awake, they give off a scent like new leaves. Asleep, they smell of upturned roots, still moist with clinging soil.

2. From the mouths of angels come healing waters, light, the peace and quietude of early morning. Also numbers of things less lauded: water tasting of metal or lead, wax and string, small brown moths that turn to powder when crushed.

3. The mouths of angels are useless, a sort of inscription or sign, built in the shallowness of an inscription or sign, and serving no known function, as angels speak in a visual language of their own, one borne through gesture as an effect of and within the air.

4. If angels are creatures, they are of matter and form compounded. If they are spirits, they are of form set in motion. If they are matter, they possess the principle of

change. If they are form, they possess the principle of destruction or preservation.

5. Their indivisibility, perishability.

6. The mouths of angels are a hoax made plausible by our own mouths, which we crudely attach to entities that possess neither body nor extension.

A round yellow sun hangs over the landscape dotted with unshapen stones. Either the arrangement of the stones is random, or else it is of an incomprehensible order. A blue sky stuck through with clouds the size and shape of boats. Since angels do not have bodily organs, Alexander of Hales qualifies the word of angels as a "spiritual nod." It is a nod insofar as it makes apparent what was previously hidden. In this regard the angel's nod shows a certain similarity to the exterior word of man, as the nod, in a certain sense, is the vehicle of the angel's inner word. In the distance, figures cluster on the earth like resting birds, tucking a seeping radiance within the folds of a garment radiantly plain.

The silence is bright blue, and everywhere. An angel arranges angels by order and ranking, a luminous line. They regard him with the round gaze of cattle. One at a time, he brings them forth with a movement of the hand, a hand extended toward the newer angel, the fingers of the senior angel each turned in toward the palm, forming a fist extended toward the newer angel, a fist that looks as though it might open up.

One at a time, he leans over each, pressing its head to the stone, back from the neck and deeply onto the surface of the stone, and with his thumb he creates an absence in the center of the face, a thumb-deep breach. The solid flesh moves like dough beneath the heavenly fingers: if it is of matter, it possesses the principle of change.

He digs two thumbs into the hole and opens it up, sideways, outward. And then their bodies too are penetrated by air. Their bodies too take a portion of the air away from itself and hold it within a chamber. That part of the body foreign to itself and capable, suddenly, of speaking in its place.

———————

In 1258 in Siena, Italy, an angel is said to have appeared in the town's central square during a festival honoring the sacrifice of Saint Catherine. The angel, shrouded in a pure and glorious light, is reported to have consumed in curiosity a single grape from the well-stocked banquet, and fallen over immediately, killed.

———————

A mouth is a tear in the wholeness of a being. From this moment on, he will find his breath leaking out from him continually, his body filling with the bodies of others, a circulation of others stepping in and out of the bounds of sensation. He will form the air into shapes with a meaning not his own, and he will hunger for the matter of others, transformed in the mouth into material raw and ready for reuse. In some accounts, a self comes into being with its first cry, its first utterance or gasp into a surround unmarked by its own voice. In others, a self is marked out only when it consumes living matter for the first time, asserting its own body upon the body of another and folding its life into that of its own. The mouth is a site of transformation at the boundary of inner and outer; it crushes the others up so that their thingliness can become someone else's own.

———————

The silent angel, his face smooth and markless as a piece of marble not yet shaped into statue. He sinks a whole fist into the mouths of the angels, twisting it this way and that, until the hole is large enough for the sounds of human language, for the words and full sentences. The wrist and forearm protrude from the heads of angels as he turns his fist around, creating space, and then opens it up slowly within the heads, making room for the teeth and tongue he will form from their matter.

The sun is quiet over the stones and the angels as they undergo their transformations. It will never again be so quiet in this field. The angelic mouths unmade, they have no way to gasp as the holes are put into them, as the pure and liquid tears collect around their eyes. All around them the stones are silent, the stones in the shape of whatever, in the shape of things that have no name but could, someday. Their necks each fit flush to their chosen stones, their stones cradling the necks that they may look up and out into the sky.

———————

A Benedictine in 1120 AD testified that he was visited nightly by an angel who came to bear witness to the consumption of his simple meal of apples and bread. Questioned by his abbot as to the moral purpose of these visits, the man had nothing to report, save that his observer grew angry if an attempt was made to cover up or otherwise conceal his rations, particularly if the monk strove out of modesty to obscure the view of his mouth.

———————

1. Because they are made in the shape of God, which is the shape of man and because they are man's brethren.

2. Because they measure the distance that inheres within man himself, as do the beasts.

3. Because the body of the word and the body of the stone are not the same thing, or because they are.

4. Because an angel is said to perish from taking human food, when a man dies of choking we say that he has received a holy death, heralding his joyful passage into realms higher and more glorious.

5. The saliva of an angel is said to improve the quality of matter and raise it to a state of greater perfection, much as the saliva of man is said to degrade it, and it is reported that a mealy apple thus inserted into the mouth of an angel and stored there for a time shall emerge fresh and devoid of flaws when it is drawn back out.

6. Because the thing and the thought are not one, or because they are.

———————

The angels mill about in the fields, picking things up from off the ground and sticking them in their mouths. The cattle regard them in passivity, and wonder. An angel discovers a small pebble and places it within the cavity. He extracts it, and behold: a pebble of the same size, shape, and specification—but now composed of solid gold. An angel regards a small flower, and plucks it from the ground. He places it in his mouth and, lo: what he removes from his mouth is no flower, but a single word. He holds the word up before the eyes of the other angels and they rejoice, marveling in the miracle of flesh made abstract. They pass the word from angel to angel, holy hand to holy hand, turning it over in their palms and observing it from every angle. The sun weighs on them from overhead, weighs like light upon them all, as they tilt their faces up toward the source, mouths open, joyful, and light touches the backs of their mouths, the unbroken backs of their throats.

Works Cited

Durandus of Saint-Pourçain, *Durandi a Sancto Porciano in Petri Lombardi Sententias Theologicas Commentarium*, book 4. Venice, 1579; reprint, Ridgewood, NJ: Gregg Press, 1964.

Iribarren, Isabel, and Martin Lenz. *Angels in Medieval Philosophical Inquiry: Their Function and Significance.* Burlington, VT: Ashgate, 2008.

Rabbit Starvation

On the first day comes the new shipment of cotton balls, bundled in blocks and factory-wrapped, masses of plastic-trapped white that hit the floor with half as much sound as expected. On that day, we begin again: plunging long knives through the blocks, cutting straight lines along the top and sides. Cotton balls sputter from slits we stanch with our hands while we cut them free. The next day we sort. At the cotton ball factory they strive to make them all the same, but variation creeps into the shapes, some barely larger, some barely lacking. Their near-uniformity makes the differences more startling. We search the mounds for ugly ones, the ones whose variance disgusts us.

This cotton ball is fine. So is the next. The next after that suffers from a deformity, a small tuft of fluff strung out like a tail. I set it aside for mending. The next is all right, and the next.

But the cotton ball after that has something wrong with it, more wrong than we've ever seen. On a white table in this spotless room sits a puff of white with a bright red blotch, an urgent liquid color soaking the center of a dry nothing.

We gather around, afraid to touch the spot with our gloves, afraid of the color lingering on our suits.

Cotton ball after cotton ball, all stained, arriving on the conveyor belt and falling off into a basket with the clean ones. Color everywhere. We look toward the cotton heap growing redder. We look toward the reddening heap knowing that one of us will need to go into it and discover what is leaking.

———————

The rabbits are white, and when I stack them they stay put, looking back at me from a creamy vagueness dotted with eyes. Rabbits are edible. They have bony bodies beneath the fleeciest fur, like whisked clouds or something even lighter. Dozens on dozens shuffle across the floor in short bursts, hopping weakly then growing tired, making the sound of teeth sinking into marshmallow. Press an ear to a rabbit mouth and hear a soft chuffing, a machinery made of cotton.

I tried everything else before I tried rabbit, and that is to my credit, I think. I've tried to eat the walls (white plaster), the floor (white plaster), and the patches of Astroturf against which their tender shapes contrast so nicely. I tried to eat dust and dew, my own fingernails and hair. As little as there is, there is enough. There is enough, and also too little, a deficit that hangs here like an overhead light. It shows the inadequacy of myself to this room, of this room to myself, of the rabbits to each other as protection or company. Even the Astroturf seems to long for something more, though what it gets is more rabbits. The sky stretches empty overhead, and I devote time to wishing something into it, a cloud or a series of them, something to watch change and improve—or rather, just change.

This room has the look of a snapshot. It slides away day by day, though not for the rabbits, who seem to multiply mathematically rather than biologically, increasing their numbers even without nourishment. This is one of the things that leads me to say aloud, though of course there is no one to listen: Hunger is, in and of itself, an eye pointed continually at what is lacking and how badly.

———————

What to feed this baby? I thought to myself. This produced no results, so I said it aloud. The baby rolled around vaguely, grabbing at its own nose, swaddled in a fair number of dishrags. It burbled in an incompetent way. I thought to myself: I am better than it, both at grabbing and articulating sounds. Then I wondered again about what to feed the baby.

The baby had been assigned to me by the government, or by a similarly well-organized group with a voice that sounded very much like that of the government. They called to tell me to come to the bus station to pick it up, and that I would have to bring my own container. They also said: clothes, bring clothes, it is not guaranteed that your baby will come clothed. My parents were disappointed in the extreme: I was only twenty years of age. "Twenty years old with a baby," my father said, grudgingly crocheting a yellow beanie on the couch. "And with so much left unlived."

Look at its teeth, I thought to myself. You can tell what anything eats if you look at its teeth. An archaeologist can look at a single tooth, even a fragment of a tooth, and find signs as to whether the tooth's owner was an agriculturalist or a hunter-gatherer. Small cavities, or caries, on the surface of the tooth indicate that carbohydrates and sugars have dissolved on its surface. Similarly, chewing on tough seeds and husks leaves wear and tear on the crowns. I looked into the baby's mouth. I was not sure it had teeth.

The baby threw up a small amount of orangish substance, which I took to mean it was full, or at least not empty, at which point I decided the question of feeding the baby could wait until I had watched a couple hours of television.

———————

Skin and slaughter the rabbits, clean the rabbits with tools made of rabbit. Stow bits in larger bits of rabbit and try to tie the package up. Tidy up and sweep matter toward the other corner. Lie supine. Lie prostrate. Pick at the Astroturf with a fingernail. Is it held there with glue? Stack the rabbits. Number the rabbits. Place a fingertip on the nose and stroke from forehead over spine to the tip of its adorable puff. Regret and regroup. Enumerate the possibilities. Write messages to the sky. The most pliant and stationary of the rabbits, the rabbits most suited to lying still as if on a page, the sort of rabbits that seem somehow to understand that lying still may be a form of self-defense, the only form. Messages spelled out in white on the white surface are nearly illegible, but spelling them out offers a one-dimensional sort of relief, like speaking to yourself in a loud and confident voice.

The line between what is already food and what will not be is either rigid or soft. I know with certainty that it exists. In moments of extremity, it glows like a bar of neon light. Sometimes its bounds are decided by my body, stubborn, for example, in the coughing up of a milky paste of plaster and false grass. It leaves a lack inside like a knot that refuses to dissolve or digest, a knot lodged a bit too high in the chest, pressing against the lungs and heart as they try to push themselves out.

You can also live an entire life thinking something inedible until, one day, you find yourself gnawing on it, like a person still asleep.

Captain Robert Falcon Scott sat in a small sled hauled by dogs, headed for a far distal point. He was to travel from the shore at one end of Antarctica to the geographic South Pole, the point at which the earth's axis of rotation meets its surface. He did this in order to become the first person to do so. It did not bother him that the earth wobbles, that the point toward which he was headed was not precise but rather a sort of consensus on where the center should be if the world were sturdy. It did not bother him that the other men complained bitterly and told each other that the number of dogs, provisions, and sleds would fail to suffice.

It did bother him, somewhat, that his was not the only party headed toward the pole, and that Amundsen's crew was rumored to be both hardy and well-supplied. Scott's men groaned.

"In a world in which the number of firsts available to mankind grows ever more paltry . . . ," Captain Robert Falcon Scott said to the crunch of ice and gasping of the dogs, the sound of air emptying from lungs, "the accomplishment of firstness is sufficient reward in and of itself. . . . We shall have salted pork for supper. . . . I am afraid the return journey is going to be dreadfully tiring and monotonous."

Earlier on, the rabbits were tame. Later, it became clear where they stood in relation to myself, in our tiny food chain of only two links—theirs and mine. When I turned my back, the rabbits would become curious, move closer, encamp themselves in the crook of my knee or elbow. They scattered as soon as I looked at them directly, fleeing to the corners, where they piled seven or eight high, climbing one another, each trying to be the farthest from me. Our fear of each other was asymptotic: time eked out a flattening in how much we could care about killing or being killed, eating or being eaten, and this numbness was a way of understanding each other. We gave up in order to know more. And so I fell asleep and would wake beneath a cover of rabbits, eat rabbit while rabbits played around me, and care for them, keeping them clean and giving them names I would immediately forget.

Experts claim that starvation differs from hunger in several respects. As the stomach begins to atrophy, the phenomenal experience of hunger grows milder, less urgent, even as the chances for acquiring food to cure the nutritional deficit grow slim. "Some think a man will die sooner if he eats continually of fat-free meat than if he eats nothing, but this is a belief on which sufficient evidence for a decision has not been gathered," wrote Canadian explorer Vilhjalmur Stefansson. In many ways, I am better suited to answer this question than anyone else, which makes me an expert in rabbit starvation. But as I become more knowledgeable, there is less I can say, shifting between a dizzying sense of freedom and a dizzying sense of sickness. In this way, starvation is not altogether unlike thinking, insofar as both processes leave the subject feeling less full, progressively, at all times.

———————

I had a dream I was lying in a very soft bed on a very soft pillow and around me was a blanket that I was chewing on, absently, like a baby chews on its own thumb, but when I woke up I found it was a rabbit I was chewing on, or rather a couple of rabbits, and I felt embarrassed, but mostly tired.

On the open tundra you can see someone approaching from five to ten miles away, dependent on weather conditions, the elevation of the viewer, and the curvature of the earth. Once you see them beginning to approach, you discover it takes forever for them to arrive. Early on, the slowness of their progress put me in a fever state. Who might it be? When they make themselves known, what will they say? Are they the threat I have been watching for? There was nothing to do from this position but ask oneself over and over again: What could that be, making its way so slowly from the horizon to my burrow? Will they arrive? Will they change course? A diet of questions is a steady way to shed weight, and health, and contentment. Now I know that it will not make a difference who it is, which is an attitude that takes the edge off but does not at all alter the fact that this edge is connected to a knife. The sky is blue as always, and today it is scored by a small figure heading toward me—with supplies? With word from the experts at the central base? With a flag to plant at my feet?

Knowing is a weak food, and watching is a weak food, and a figure on the horizon is a weak food destined to weaken with knowledge, as at all times we walk on a thin layer, tread our way toward the far reach, and so on.

You, Disappearing

When I went downstairs this morning and found Cookie missing, I knew that official emergency procedure called for me to phone all the information in to the Bureau of Disappearances. At the prompting of the prerecorded voice, I would enter my social security number and zip code. I would press 2 to report the sudden absence of an animal, 3 for "domestic animal," and then at the sound of the tone I would speak the word "cat" clearly and audibly into the telephone receiver. The woman's voice would then give a short parametric definition of a cat, and if this definition matched my missing item, I could press the pound sign to record a fifteen-second description. A three-note melody would let me know that my claim had been filed, and then that lovely prerecorded voice would read out my assigned case number, along with some instructions on how to update or cancel my claim.

Instead, I picked up the phone and pushed your number into it. I was always telling you about problems you couldn't fix, as though multiplying badness could dilute it.

Cookie's gone, I said, and waited for your response.

. . .

There was a pause on the other end of the line.

Have you phoned it in? you asked. Your voice was casual, like it was someone else's pet entirely, a pet from a faraway land owned by people we'd never meet.

I didn't, I said. I'm kind of depressed, I added. I was often depressed, but now we all had better reasons to be.

I'm sorry, you said back.

Cookie loved to chew on wires, I said.

I know, you said. You didn't say you wished you could be here. I didn't say it either.

There was nothing more to say. I hung up the phone. Sometimes I dialed you back right away just to hear you pick up and know that your hands were, at that very moment, resting on a chunk of plastic that threaded its way delicately to me over hundreds of miles of wire and cord. To know that even though your voice had disappeared, you had not yet. But recently I hadn't been allowing myself any callbacks. I was getting more afraid of the day when you wouldn't pick up.

————————

The apocalypse was quiet. It had a way about it, a certain charm. It could be called graceful. It was taking a long time.

. . .

People prepared for an apocalypse that they could take up arms against, bunker down with. People hoarded filtered water, canned corn, dry milk, batteries. They published books on how to get things done in the new postworld, a world that they always imagined as being much like our own, only missing one or two key things. They might imagine, for example, that survivors would reemerge onto a planet stripped of all vegetable and plant life. First, the animals would grow vicious and then starve. It would be important to hoard as many of these animals as possible, pack them in salt and hide them away to keep. You'd want to have a supply of emergency seed to grow in a secure location, maybe using sterilized soil that you had already hoarded. Then you'd want to gather a crew. One muscleman with a heart of gold, a scientist type, an engineer, a child, and somebody that you thought maybe you could love, if you survived long enough to love them.

Nobody thought the apocalypse would be so polite and quirky. Things just popped out of existence, like they had forgotten all about themselves. Now when you misplaced your keys, you didn't go looking for them. Maybe you went to your landlord and asked for the spare set, took them to the hardware store and made two copies this time, an extra in case the disappearing wasn't a one-off but part of a trend. Or maybe you took this as a sign and decided to leave instead, walked out directionless into the world to find your own vanishing point, which meant moving to Chicago to stay with your brother, who still had the keys to his house and a spare set to give to you.

· · ·

It was cute the way this apocalypse zapped things out of existence, one by one. It was so clean and easy, like clicking on a little box to close an Internet browser window. It had a sense of humor: a fat man walking down the street lined with small abandoned shops would look down and find that his trousers had vanished, baring his out-of-season Halloween boxers to the public. That kind of humor.

Videos of things like this used to show up all the time on the Internet, until the Internet went.

———————

I thought I would visit the Ferris wheel at the pier before it vanished. I didn't know when it would go. I had the idea that I could try to be the last person ever to visit it, but that would require a lot of work, a lot of waiting around and watching, and there were things to do even in the time of last things. I put two apples in a plastic bag and headed out the door, which I didn't lock even though it would have been easy to do. I took the elevator down to the first floor and walked on East Jackson Drive to the edge of the water, then up along the highway, holding onto the handrail with one gloved hand. A sedan full of teenagers drove by, and one of them shouted a blurry word at me that sounded like it had once been a taunt. It was winter, but it wasn't so cold. There was less weather, the same way there was less of everything. This day resembled the day before: sleepy air and wan blue sky, no clouds but a vague foggy white that might just have been a thinning of the atmosphere.

At the pier I saw the seagulls huddling together on the boardwalk, pressing their dirty white bodies up against each other. They seemed able to eat anything—crusts, rinds, paper napkins. They were made to survive, even in a fading world that was unthinking itself faster than we could fill it back up with our trash. One seagull worked to swallow a little plastic toy lion, snapping its beak down on it with blunt patience. The Ferris wheel loomed up big behind them at the end of the pier, though it wasn't as big as it had seemed the first time I saw it. The wheel was missing spokes at random, and some of the red seating cars had gone. It looked like the mouth of someone who had been punched over and over again in the face.

I walked over to it, right out in the open, but nobody saw me. When I reached the base the controls were all locked up. It had a big goofy lever that you could set to different speeds, like in a cartoon. I ducked the chain and climbed into the ground-level car, the one in starting position, and staggered from one side of the car to the other to try to make it swing, but it wasn't any fun. Then I sat facing the water and put down the guardrail. The lake licked at the shore the way it used to. When water disappears, other water rushes in right away to take its place, you never see any kind of hole or gap. Then when I reached into my plastic bag, I only had one apple.

. . .

This apocalypse disappears objects of all kinds, and it swallows memories whole too. I didn't want to be around you when you forgot me. I didn't want to watch it fall out of your head so easily, I was hoping to forget you first. But sometimes I second-guessed that. Then I called you and tried to be angry, as though you were the one who had been so afraid of being forgotten that you needed to move out of the apartment, out of the city, and into another city where nothing had any familiarity to start with, or any familiarity to lose. I thought you might have forgotten who did what to whom, but you haven't yet.

————————

When the first things began to disappear, it had looked funny, like a continuity slip-up in a bad movie. You and I would make sound effects for them, shouting "Poof!" or "Boink!" as some flowers blinked themselves out of existence. This was how we'd make each other laugh. In those days the world still looked full, even though it was emptying fast. Then too many things vanished to keep making the sounds: we saw it was sad that anything in the world had gone and could not return. You joked around, saying there'd be fewer chores, our lives would clean up after themselves for a change, but still you went on doing the dishes, vacuuming the little spaces around and under the furniture, putting on a fresh shirt every day, making the bed. You folded cups out of paper for us to drink from when the glasses went away, and when the paper went you used the nice cloth napkins, which worked badly. You were the sort of person that keeps it all going, and I was the other kind.

This became clear two weeks after the first vanishings, when the news stations named it "The Disappocalypse." On the day they called it irreversible, I walked out of the office just before lunch. I didn't tell anyone where I was going, I didn't reply to the e-mails asking whether we wanted to cancel our health insurance and cash out retirement plans. I knew I wouldn't be coming back. The subway was shut down so I walked all the way to our apartment on Myrtle Avenue, across the Brooklyn Bridge to the Flatbush Extension. On that day the world still felt crowded. The sky above was pure undiluted blue, thick enough to mask how much emptiness lay behind it, out past the atmosphere. Cars were lined up on the bridge, bumper to bumper. Drivers honked sporadically, without aggression, like migrating geese.

When I got home, it was late afternoon and you'd be back by six thirty. I tried reading the newspaper, but I'd read all I could stand about the vanishing, and the other sections had been thinning out, some with blank patches nobody bothered to fill where the color of the paper showed through grayish and soft. Then it was seven thirty, and eight, and still you weren't around. I gave Cookie her dry food and refilled her water. I started crying and stopped again and then dragged eyeliner back over my lids so that I looked the way I had before. When you showed up, it was close to nine, and you smelled normal: no sweat, no cigarettes, no liquor. Where had you been? You had been working late. Hadn't you heard?

They said "irreversible," "imminent," "end of days." They used those words.

I put wet marks into your shirt as you held me. Then when I pulled away your chest looked back at me with two blurry eyes.

Why did you do that? I asked. Why were you away so long?

I was working, you said. A lot of people have left, you know that. Toby and Marianne and all of the interns. We're understaffed. I'm on two new building projects. Your back was warm and real under my hands.

There's nothing to build, I said. The world is going.

I know that, you replied. But there isn't anything we can do about it.

That's what I'm saying, I said.

I looked at you looking at me. I heard that we were saying the same thing, though I didn't understand how it was possible for us to mean it so differently. Later that night I asked you to quit your job too, stay home with me during the days. We could get survival-ready, rent a garden-level apartment with barricadable windows. We could walk around all day getting to know the things that wouldn't be there for much longer. But you wouldn't. You liked being an architect. You said it would make you happy to have added even one thing to a world now headed for total subtraction.

The walking path next to the highway passed under a bridge. In the cool dark beneath was a bench facing onto some empty lot full of broken glass from bottles that people had thrown just because. When sunlight hit the broken pieces, the ground lit up like a reverse chandelier, a glittering patch of green and white. Now there was less each time I walked by. Also, no bench. I stood there facing the glass, eating my last apple.

There had been times when I thought I might be with you indefinitely, something approaching an entire life. But then when there was only a finite amount of time, a thing we could see the limit of, I wasn't so sure. I didn't know how to use a unit of time like this, too long for a game of chess or a movie but so much shorter than we had imagined. It felt like one of those days when we woke up too late for breakfast and lay in bed until it was too late for lunch. Those days made me nervous. On those days we fought about how to use our time. You didn't want to live your life under pressure, as though we'd run out, as though it were the last days. I'm not ill, you said. We aren't dying, we don't have cancer, you said. So I don't want to live like we do, you said. There are two kinds of people, and one of them will give up first.

. . .

When we fought, you got over it first. I'd watch you from the kitchen, through a rectangular space cut into the wall, and I could see you studying the newspaper, ducking your head down to read small details in the photographs. I saw how gracefully you fell back into whatever article you had been reading before. Even then I knew: whatever hollow I made in you if I left would heal up like a hole sunk into water, quick as water rushing to fill some passing wound.

This far from the pier I could still hear the seagulls fighting over scraps, crying out with their harsh voices. Sounds carried farther these days, tearing through the thin air like a stone thrown as hard as you can toward the sea. The bitten-down apple core wet my right-hand glove, while with the other hand I pressed on the bridge of my nose. There are two kinds of people: one will only weep when the possibility exists, however remote, that someone will hear them. I put the core of the apple down on the ground and looked at it. Poof, I said. I waited for something to happen. Then I went and walked back up the path toward the high-rise.

When I got home, I collected all of Cookie's toys, her food bowl and water bowl, the little purple ball with a bell in it, the stuffed squeaking duck that was almost her size. I lined them all up on the mantel in the living room so that I could watch them disappear, one after the other.

———————

Was the disappearing growing faster every day? No. Was it moving geographically from west to east, or east to west? Was it vanishing the world alphabetically, taxonomically, or in chronological order? It wasn't. As hard as we tried to understand it, there didn't seem to be much order to the disappearing at all. A week would go by with everything pretty much in its proper place, and then all of a sudden there was no such thing as magazines, not in your home or anyone else's, and nobody to bother making new ones. Did it work its way down from the biggest things to the smallest? Was there a plan? When you were in the right mood, when you were too tired to care much, it was beautiful—like watching the house across the street as someone walked through it turning each of the lights off in order, one by one, for the night.

I sat on the floor of my brother's empty living room and ate four chocolate chip granola bars in a row. I had already called you once today, but I was working on a reason to call you again. Experts suggested that the things disappearing most quickly now might be intangible, metaphysical: concepts, memories, and modes of thought were just as vulnerable to erasure, they said, though they couldn't give any concrete examples. I thought I'd better call you to see if you still remembered that Cookie had gone.

. . .

I pushed the buttons in order. It rang twice, and then I heard you.

Hello? you said.

It's me, I said.

It's you, you said back to me.

I just wanted to call to see if you still remembered Cookie, I said.

Of course I still remember Cookie, you said.

There was silence on both our ends, a blur of static on the line between us.

What do you remember? I asked.

I remember that you picked her because she bit you, you said, and you decided it was important that you win this one animal over. I remember you didn't know how to hold a cat at the beginning, so you grabbed her just anywhere. You grabbed her in the middle and tried to pick her up that way. You got bit a lot, you added.

I have your number memorized, I said.

That's good, you said.

. . .

And I said I should let you go, and you said good night and we hung up on each other.

I missed you more now than I had when I lost you. I was forgetting the bad things faster than I forgot the good, and the changing ratio felt a little bit like falling in love even though I was actually speaking to you less and less. I used to play a game I called "Are We Going to Make It?" You were playing too, whether you knew it or not. It worked like this: you'd forget that we were going to see the movie together and you'd go by yourself instead or with a friend, while I waited at home. Or you'd stay at work until four in the morning and forget to charge your phone, and you'd wake me up on the couch where I had fallen asleep trying to stay up for you. Then I would ask myself: Are We Going to Make It? And the next thing, whatever thing you did next, would become the answer, a murky thing that I'd study until I was too tired to think about it anymore.

An "independent physicist" living in Arizona had become famous for his theories on how the Disappearing might be a sort of existential illusion, analogous to an optical illusion. He said the fact that we still remember what's been taken and can picture it in our minds is proof that it still exists. It's like how you only see the duck or the bunny at a given moment, never both, he said. Only imagine that instead of knowing the bunny exists alongside your experience of the duck, you believe that it's been irrevocably lost. It's all about vantage point, he said, temporal vantage point: the way you might lose sight of your house when you drive away from it, but find it again when you look for it from the top of a hill. To think your house was lost, he said, would be loony. Disappeared things were like this, he said, coexistent but obscured in time. This was his theory of spatiotemporal obstruction. Those who believed in it believed that there was one special place that offered temporal "higher ground." They made pilgrimages to a particular beach in Normandy where the cliffs were chalky white, the color of doves, and where it was rumored that recently disappeared things sometimes reappeared, soft-edged and worn and looking thirty or forty years older. In 1759 a twelve-year-old girl was said to have drowned herself there to avoid marriage to a much older man.

I sat on the floor and put the granola bar wrappers in a plastic bag. I put the plastic bag inside another plastic bag. Plastic bags were disappearing too, but my brother had had so many of them to begin with. Then I picked up the phone to call you back. I put your number in from memory.

Instead of you, I heard an error song and a recorded voice telling me my call could not be completed.

I dialed the Bureau of Disappearances. At the prompt, I pressed 1 for "person," then 1 again for "male." I pressed 3 to indicate "age twenty-one to thirty." Then I was supposed to press 3 for "friend," but instead I pressed 2 for "lover or significant other." I hoped you wouldn't mind. The beautiful female voice declared you a "male lover between the ages of twenty-one and thirty" and asked if that was correct. I pressed the pound key and then I described you.

———————

I remember it was a bright morning in the fall and I woke onto your face looking in on mine. Some mornings when we woke together we pretended that one of us had forgotten who the other was. One of us had become an amnesiac. That one would ask: Who are you? Where am I? and it was the other's job to make up a new story. A good story was long, and the best stories could make me feel like I had gotten a whole second life, a bonus one. Yellow leaves outside the window threw yellowish light on the sheets as you told me not to worry. I was safe, I was with you. We had been living together since grad school; we met on the hottest day of the year, near the gondolas in the middle of the park. We were sitting on benches facing the pond and eating the same kind of sandwich, turkey and swiss in a spinach wrap.

But that's what actually happened, I said.

I know, you said, making a fake guilty face.

In the fall afternoon, leaves fell off whenever they fell off: it didn't depend on their color or weight or the force of the wind outdoors.

You added: I just couldn't think of anything.

. . .

The disappearing when it started happening was everywhere, subtly, it hung on our days the way a specific hour
does on a moment, dragging it down and reminding you of
how much time you've let pass. It was a flavor you woke up
with in your mouth, like the taste of blood on a dry winter
morning. This made leaving easier in the moments before I
had realized what I was planning to do. I stood outside our
building with no keys, and I was calling you over and over
on the cell phone even though I knew you were at work.
Each time I got your voice mail I imagined that you had
vanished, until one time I imagined that you had vanished
and I didn't feel any way about it. It was like I had disappeared. I saw the things continuing on without me, and I
didn't mind. I went to the ATM on the corner and pulled
everything out of my checking account. Checking accounts
were still around then, existing invisibly somewhere. Possibly they exist still, even though the banks went. I took
the cash and our car and got on the highway, driving on
I-80 west toward Chicago. If it hadn't been the End of Days,
would we still be together? The most difficult thing about
leaving you was discovering that I went on: that I had to be
there sixteen hours a day watching myself live my own life,
that I had to stay near myself all the time as I asked myself
question after question, that I had to sit there in my body
and watch the phone ring over and over next to me that
night, after you had gotten home.

After the announcement, people did one of two things.
Either they tried to care more, or they tried caring less.

They decided to survive, to collect and hide and ration, or they decided to let the amount of time left in their lives work away at them. They tried to grow vegetables in their small backyards or they let the yard get overgrown, falling asleep drunk in the afternoon on a lawn chair encircled by weeds. For a while we did whatever we had chosen with dedication. But it was difficult to stay dedicated for more than a few weeks, and eventually we middled, caring about things sloppily and in spurts. We poked at the dirt and then fell asleep, feeling that we should have done more or maybe less. In the end, there was only one kind of person.

In the master bedroom I turned down the sheets. My brother wouldn't be back again, but I made the bed every day to be a good guest. I made it the hotel way, everything tucked in, the sheets stretched tight across the mattress and leaving no room to shift or wrinkle. Sleeping in it meant that you had to tear it all apart. I yanked the pillows out from underneath the blankets, pulled the sheets down to the foot of the bed, let the comforter fall to the floor. Then I climbed in.

I have one of the last working phones, I said out loud.

I had started sleeping with the lights on: I wanted more minutes of seeing, more things I could see if I happened to open my eyes. Outside the window there was snow falling, falling like movie snow, all the dreamy fluffy bits drifting around in the light of a single streetlamp. I wished that I loved the woman on the Disappearance hotline so that I could call and hear her voice anytime I wanted, and feel that feeling that it didn't seem I'd be feeling again. Whoever loved her was lucky, if they were still around. I watched the snow slow down, thin out. Then it was two or three pieces at a time, falling reversibly, wavering up and down and up again like they didn't know where to go.

The light stayed on for a few minutes. I saw my reflection in the window. Then the bulb blanked out overhead. In the dark I could hear the cord swinging empty above, but I saw nothing. I knew from the mounting silence that other things were vanishing too. They say everything in the world vibrates at its own specific frequency, each thing releases a tiny bit of sound. But nothing, nothing, doesn't vibrate at all. I felt the heat radiating from my body with no place to go. Dots of darkness that weren't really there drifted past my eyes. How would I know I was vanishing if there were nobody around to see me? What would tell me that I wasn't just falling asleep? In the darkness I couldn't see the disappearing any longer but I knew it was all going, going far far away. Until gradually I didn't even know that anymore.

There was a woman in Lincoln, Nebraska, who claimed to be able to communicate with the disappeared. You could call her on the telephone and tell her who you were looking for, their full name, how old, how tall, how heavy. She would go out to the old well behind her house, a well that her grandfather had built decades earlier, and shout that information deep down into it. In the echo that came back they said you could hear whispers from the other side, your loved ones grabbing and molding the shouted words, distorting them to say what they needed said. You had to pay her in real gold, jewelry or bullion: it had to gleam. She wished we could hear their voices as she did, how happy they are, how they miss us. She said that everything that disappeared from our side went over to theirs, where they kept living normal lives, waiting for the things still lingering with us to join them, and make the world whole once more.

Acknowledgments

These stories were written in different places at different times, and they hold traces of so many different people that this acknowledgments page could become a never-ending list. Thank you to Claudia Ballard for having faith in me, for being there for me, for being able to see right into a story and point at its heart. Thank you to my editor, Terry Karten, for her vision, penetrating intelligence, and support, and to Heather Drucker, Cal Morgan, Laura Brown, Jillian Verrillo, and the rest of the team at Harper for working so hard for this book. Thank you to Barry Harbaugh for believing in me better than I could myself.

Thank you to Bard College, where I finished this collection and was amazed by the people around me. To Cheryl and John at VCCA France, where I wrote and also was a healthy organism, and to the Bread Loaf Writers Conference for being a magical place. Thank you to Robert Coover, Thalia Field, Nicholas Christopher, Heidi Julavits, Ben Marcus, Sam Lipsyte, Eric Chinski, and Rivka Galchen, who taught. To Lorin Stein, Bradford Morrow, Micaela Morrissette, Michael Ray, Andrew Bourne, Meakin Armstrong, and Willing Davidson, who edited. Thank you to Kathleen Alcott, JW McCormack, Shayne Barr, Kimberly Wang, Benjamin Hale, Jameelah Lang, Ariel

Lewiton, Kara Gilvarry, Gwen Osborne, and Shawn Wen, who did some of everything. Thank you to my parents who loved me the whole time. And thank you to Alex Gilvarry, my first reader and favorite writer, the ideal person to love.

About the Author

ALEXANDRA KLEEMAN is a writer and scholar. She is the author of *You Too Can Have a Body Like Mine*, winner of the 2016 Bard Fiction Prize, and her short fiction has appeared in *The New Yorker, The Paris Review, Zoetrope: All-Story, Conjunctions, BOMB, Gulf Coast*, and *Guernica*. Her nonfiction has appeared in *Harper's, Tin House, ELLE*, and *n+1*. She received her MFA in fiction from Columbia University, and has received grants and scholarships from the Bread Loaf Writers Conference, the Virginia Center for the Creative Arts, and the Santa Fe Art Institute. She lives in Staten Island.

A Note on the Type

This book is set in Walbaum. Justus Erich Walbaum designed the Walbaum font in 1804. Originally punchcut in Weimar, the designer was inspired by other Modern Didone typefaces that had been created, such as Bodoni and Didot. Its extreme vertical stress, and fine hairlines contrasted with bold main strokes are typical of Modern fonts, yet Walbaum has many unique character quirks that make it open, warm, and very graceful. It is considered to be the most important specifically German example of neo-classicist type. Jan Tschichold described it as "the most beautiful German version" of modern type.